Shadow at Sun Lake

Herald Press Books by Esther Bender

Katie and the Lemon Tree
Shadow at Sun Lake
April Bluebird

Shadow at Sun Lake

Esther Bender

HERALD PRESS
Scottdale, Pennsylvania
Waterloo, Ontario

Library of Congress Cataloging-in-Publication Data

Bender, Esther, 1942-
　　Shadow at Sun Lake / Esther Bender.
　　　　p. cm.
　　Summary: Timid Cassie is always in the shadow of her best
friend Sheila, but when they spend the summer at Sun Lake,
it's Cassie who takes the lead in searching out mysterious
reports of panthers in the woods.
　　ISBN 0-8361-9007-6 (trade pbk. : acid-free paper)
　　1. Camping—Fiction. [1. Courage—Fiction. 2. Self-
acceptance—Fiction. 3. Friendship—Fiction. 4. Panthers—
Fiction.]
I. Title.
PZ7.B43137Sh 1995
[Fic]—dc20
　　　　　　　　　　　　　　　　　　　　　　　94-33947
　　　　　　　　　　　　　　　　　　　　　　　CIP
　　　　　　　　　　　　　　　　　　　　　　　AC

The paper used in this publication is recycled and meets the mini-
mum requirements of American National Standard for Information Sciences—Permanence of Paper for Printed Library Materials,
ANSI Z39.48-1984.

In chapter 6, Acts 10:28 is quoted from KJV/NRSV.

SHADOW AT SUN LAKE
Copyright © 1995 by Herald Press, Scottdale, Pa. 15683
　　Published simultaneously in Canada by Herald Press,
　　Waterloo, Ont. N2L 6H7. All rights reserved
Library of Congress Catalog Number: 94-33947
International Standard Book Number: 0-8361-9007-6
Printed in the United States of America
Book design by Gwen M. Stamm
Cover art by Susan Graber Hunsberger

04 03 02 01 00 99 98 97 96 95 10 9 8 7 6 5 4 3 2 1

To John Davies,
builder of the lake,
the setting for
this work of fiction

Contents

1 Leaving Washington

" '. . . also called a mountain lion, cougar, panther, or puma.' "

The words hung in the air. Cassie Valin, waking in the back seat of the car, caught their echo. Her best friend, Sheila Jordan, was in front, reading to the driver, Sheila's mother. The radio whispered.

The noon heat of the sun and the vibration of the car window against Cassie's forehead annoyed her. She jerked her pillow upward without opening her eyes, mashed it into the corner beside the window, and tried to go back to sleep without thinking of her tight sweaty clothes.

Cassie wondered why she had let Sheila talk her into wearing old jeans. She was nearly two inches taller than last year. Her pant legs were too short, and her belt pinched when she slumped in the seat.

She'd wanted to wear the new comfortable clothes Mom had bought her. But Sheila had almost thrown a fit: "I'll just *die* if you wear those floppy things. *Your* legs always look tan, but *mine* look like flour. And you can't wear *new* clothes to *camp!* Real campers don't wear *new clothes!* You'll look like a *tourist!*"

The way she said *tourist* made Cassie sure she didn't want to be one. She sighed. Sheila was so beautiful! Cassie thought her own brown eyes and curly hair were plain. If she had Sheila's long, straight blonde hair and blue eyes, . . . if she were half as popular as Sheila, . . . if she *were* Sheila . . .

A newspaper rustled and snapped in the front seat with Sheila's growing excitement. "Listen to this, Mom! 'Cougars on the East Coast are like four-legged UFOs. The official viewpoint of the federal and state governments is that they don't exist.' That's it! That's what I'll do, Mom. When I'm a biologist, I'll prove they *do* exist."

The turn signals ticked and the car surged into passing gear. Mrs. Jordan chuckled, but Cassie didn't hear her answer.

Sheila read on. " 'To report cougar sightings, call the twenty-four-hour, toll-free hotline in Baltimore.' Mom! Do you think there are cougars at Sun Lake?"

Oh, no! Cassie thought. *Sheila will see cougars for sure!*

Mrs. Jordan laughed, then said, "No! We've been camping at Sun Lake for ten years and haven't even *heard* of any. And you don't have to decide on your life work now. Yesterday you wanted to be a beautician, today a biologist."

Sheila a biologist? Cassie thought of the time when Sheila had the whole school looking for a snake she saw slither away in the storage room. It turned out to be Bobby Bristol's rubber snake. They found it in his desk, but not before the whole school was in an uproar. Sheila didn't mind. She thrived on attention.

Mrs. Jordan was humming to herself. Her husband called her Peggy, but Cassie couldn't call a teacher "Peggy." Without looking, Cassie could see her slender hands curled around the steering wheel. Her nails would be manicured and polished.

Sheila's mother was an art teacher and an artist who painted in both water colors and acrylics. Cassie often wondered how she could keep her hands so lovely, day after day.

The paper rustled again, then Sheila burst out, " 'Ghost of the forest.' Mom, this says, 'The Indians called the cougar the ghost of the forest. If the cougar doesn't *want* you to know he's there, you *won't* know he's there.' "

Ghost of the forest! Cassie didn't believe in ghosts, but it was easy to imagine a cougar as a ghost. It might hypnotize her with its eyes. It might snarl and attack her. It might be an evil spirit.

She shivered, then told herself, *Now that's silly. A cougar is just another animal, not an evil spirit!* But she couldn't help thinking of a book she had seen in the bookstore. On the cover was a ruby-eyed black cat that bared its teeth above a tombstone.

Sheila's voice broke into her thoughts. "Here it says 'big cats could be traveling up and down the Appalachian range.' "

"Well, maybe you and Cassie will have the summer of your life. Maybe you'll see a cougar," Mrs. Jordan joked.

Sheila's voice dropped to a husky whisper, "I just

know Cassie'll get homesick. Remember my slumber party, when we took her home?"

"That was three years ago," Mrs. Jordan reminded her. "She'll be fine. Being with us is certainly better than staying in that hot apartment in D.C."

Cassie's cheeks burned. Sheila was talking about *her*. Three years ago, after Dad left and right after the divorce, Cassie had been afraid Mom would leave her, too. She was over that now. Maybe Sheila hadn't noticed. Of course she could spend a summer away from Mom. *I'll show Sheila!* she thought.

A tractor trailer roared by. In its wake, Cassie caught a few more hushed words, ". . . shadow. I wish . . . I get tired of it."

Shadow? What was Sheila talking about? Cassie couldn't ask without seeming to eavesdrop. She thumped her pillow and coughed several times to let them know she was awake.

A wet, rough tongue lapped her cheek. She opened her eyes. Her black dog, a Lab named Midnight, thrust a wet nose against her neck.

"Down, Middie!" She petted the dog affectionately. Its tail immediately thumped against the stack of unpainted canvases by the other window.

Cassie smoothed out the blanket that covered the seat to keep off dog hairs, then patted her pet. Midnight settled down.

Cassie brushed back straggles of sweaty, dark-brown curls. She hated her unruly hair. Sheila called her "Mophead." The nickname reminded Cassie of the smelly mop that hung in the basement laundry room of their apartment building.

Midnight suddenly stood up and plopped herself onto Cassie's lap.

"Middie!" Cassie wailed. She shoved the dog off. How hot it was, even with the air conditioner running! Why did Middie have to be so exuberant? The heat would have turned most dogs to putty.

The dog was gazing at her soulfully. "Middie!" Cassie's voice was apologetic. She stroked the Lab's satin coat. The dog returned her affection by standing up, thrusting her nose against Cassie's neck, and doing an awkward turn in the cramped space. Once more Midnight settled down.

"You awake?" called Sheila. Her head appeared over the back of the front seat. The velour fabric of the seat caught Sheila's long, sleek hair and spread it into two fans. Sheila flashed a smile, metallic with braces. Midnight snuffled and thrust her wet nose into Sheila's face.

"Yuck!" protested Sheila, wiping away the slobber. She giggled, then addressed the dog, "I didn't ask you to kiss me. Wait till we get to Sun Lake. You're in for a surprise! The geese will pinch you if you kiss them!"

Midnight cocked her head back and forth, long ears flopping, eyes alert.

"She knows you're talking to her," Cassie interpreted wisely.

Sheila's blue eyes sparkled as she petted Midnight. "Did you ever see Mom's geese pictures? They're good! They sell well, too! Mom paints her favorite geese every summer—a pair she named Charlie and Lila."

"We're almost there!" Mrs. Jordan sang out. "Time

for the local news. I always tune in when we get close to camp."

Camp! Nine weeks in the Jordan's trailer at Sun Lake! Cassie's stomach churned. She had visited her dad and step-mom some weekends, but never before had she left Mom for nine weeks.

She pulled herself to the front of the seat to see the clock. One o'clock. Right this minute, Mom was in class, studying for her degree.

"I don't want you home alone while I'm in class all day," Mom had stated. "You're only fourteen."

"Only fourteen!" Cassie cried. "Mom! Look at me. I'm practically grown! I can stay alone."

"Grown or not, you're not staying alone. You're still so thin your knees are knobby. You only weigh a hundred-and-four. Besides, it was wonderful of the Jordans to invite you. They said you could even take Midnight, and you can come home with Mr. Jordan if you get homesick. Besides, it's the only way you'll get a vacation this summer."

Get homesick? Maybe. But Cassie knew she'd handle it. She felt ready for a challenge.

2 Unexpected Trouble

Cassie slid to the front of the seat to watch the road. Midnight wedged herself behind her mistress. Up ahead, the four-lane highway slashed through a deep cut in a rugged mountain range. Such mountains surprised her—only three hours from the nation's capital!

She and Mom seldom went beyond the school where Mom taught, the church, the grocery and department stores, Rock Creek Park, and the homes of their few friends. Mom had no time for travel since her divorce.

"After this summer . . . ," Mom would begin, then talk of going on vacation. She would end by saying, "But this summer, I must take classes toward my degree to get a pay raise."

"Thirty more miles," announced Sheila. "Oh, Cassie! We're going to have the best time. You'll meet Ace and Karen and Bill. And there is this *impressive* boy, Lyle, who cuts the grass. On Sundays, Joseph plays the fiddle and tells stories and we sing. And we eat and sleep and read and walk all the time and . . ."

Sheila chattered on while Cassie watched the road. The miles ticked away slowly. Up ahead, another mountain range grew larger.

"Next exit, ten miles," Sheila sang out, "then only two more miles to Sun Lake. Open the window, Cassie. Feel the cool! It's cooler in the mountains."

Cassie rolled down the window. Halfway up the mountain, cool air fanned her face. "Wow! You can really *feel* the temperature change!" she exclaimed. She turned up the window, shooed Midnight from behind her, and settled back.

Mrs. Jordan suddenly raised her arm and called sternly, "Listen!" She turned up the volume on the radio.

". . . the fourteenth case of rabies in the county this summer," intoned the broadcaster. "If you have a pet that has not had rabies shots this year, take it to the free clinic at the health department on Thursday—that's tomorrow, folks—Thursday between the hours of 2:00 and 6:00 P.M.

"Exercise extreme caution when approaching any animal that appears fierce or sluggish. Report any animal you *suspect* is dying from rabies. The health department warns pet owners to protect their animals and themselves when in wooded areas where ticks are prevalent. Ticks carry the dreaded Lyme disease."

"Ticks!" Cassie muttered. "You had your rabies shot, Middie. But how will I keep you from getting ticks?" Cassie's voice set the dog's tail thumping against the canvases.

"Here's our exit! We're getting off," sang Sheila. "I'm glad you're with us, Cassie. I got so bored last summer while Mom painted all day."

Mrs. Jordan's blond hair bounced as she turned her head. She laughed and teased, "Until you discovered your friends at the Dari-Treat."

"You have to admit they made life more interesting," countered Sheila.

Mrs. Jordan chuckled but didn't answer. She was checking side and rearview mirrors, guiding the car through traffic at the intersection. They passed a mini-mall, three fast-food restaurants, several motels, and a few houses. Abruptly the road narrowed.

"The Dari-Treat is right around the turn," announced Sheila. A moment later, Cassie saw a giant neon cone that marked the ice-cream restaurant.

As they passed, Sheila's voice rang out, "One more mile!" The front seat creaked as she bounced back and forth. "Here's the state forest." Now she sounded like a tour guide.

Wild grapevines twined and tangled in the trees on both sides of the narrow road, and overhead the spread-out branches nearly met.

"Like a jungle," Sheila added, "with tigers, lions, bears, elephants."

"Get serious!" Cassie protested.

"Skunks, groundhogs, squirrels, chipmunks, deer, wild turkey . . . bears."

"Bears!" It was hard to know when Sheila was telling it straight.

"Yes, they say the state stocked bears about five years ago. I've never seen any, though. There are lots of deer—whitetails. We'll go out early tomorrow morning and see some."

They left the forest as abruptly as they had entered it. Mrs. Jordan turned into a gravel drive. They coasted under a stone arch that proclaimed SUN LAKE across the top, then passed the camp office and store. Ahead was the lake. Eager to see it, Cassie hunched forward on the seat.

The water, a round looking glass, reflected the blue sky. A lacy filigree of silver-leaved trees and a gravel road made a frame around it. On the water bobbed a few sailboats and canoes. A mountain, bald on top and mottled with shades of green, formed the backdrop. Cassie hadn't expected it to be as beautiful or as quiet.

"See what I mean!" Sheila burst out proudly. "It's so quiet here a buzzing bumble bee is an event. The front lake is the round part you see, but there's another darker lake behind. The road circles between them on a causeway to that little island and across a bridge and back to the camp office. Our camper's on the island."

They inched along the gravel road, straddling shallows that would become puddles in a rain. Then they crossed the causeway and stopped before an old house trailer. It was painted a dull green and shaded by large old trees. One end faced the road.

A thick wild grapevine weighed down by a mass of Virginia creeper hung from an oak in front and draped itself across the window. The trailer looked as though it had grown roots right down through the tangled vines on the ground. Behind it, scraggly wind-warped pines scratched the sky. In front of the pines, a thicket of overgrown rhododendron blocked vision to the lake.

"This is it! Come on, Cassie," Sheila shouted.

Jumping out, she pulled Cassie's door open. Midnight shot past her.

"Wait!" called Cassie, but the dog disappeared into the rhododendron behind the trailer.

"She'll be back," Sheila assured her.

Mrs. Jordan backed the car in beside the trailer. Sheila and Cassie carried suitcases and boxes inside. Between loads, Cassie made a quick trip around the rhododendron thicket. She saw that the ground sloped down steeply from the front of the trailer to the rear, where concrete pilings held it on the level. Then she hurried back to carry in a box of groceries.

"You get the top bunk," declared Sheila as Cassie placed the food on the table opposite the bunks. Sheila pointed and said, "Clothes go in these drawers. Food in those drawers." A sliding door closed off the hallway. Another door closed off the back bedroom.

The mattresses felt soggy and smelled musty. Mrs. Jordan plugged in a small electric heater with a fan and aimed it at the bed. "The dampness and smell will soon be gone," she promised.

Fifteen minutes later, everything was unpacked and stored. The empty suitcases and boxes were returned to the car trunk. Mrs. Jordan went outside to store paint supplies in an outdoor shed.

"Let's lie in the sun," Sheila proposed.

They were in the bedroom starting to change clothes when they heard a scream.

"That's Mom!" Sheila cried. She yanked on her shirt and headed outside, with Cassie following her.

Mrs. Jordan was by the shed, yelling, "No! NO! Put it down!" Her face was white with purple around the lips. "You bad dog! PUT IT DOWN!"

Midnight stood there, proudly holding a large bird in her mouth. The long neck and the head of the fowl, black with white cheek patches, dragged on the ground. Midnight's tail wagged.

"PUT IT DOWN!" Before Mrs. Jordan's anger, the dog's pose withered and her tail curled between her legs, but she didn't give up the bird. Mrs. Jordan screamed one more time, picked up a large stiff canvas, and flailed the dog with it. Midnight dropped the bird. Whining, she crawled under the trailer.

Mrs. Jordan picked up the bird and groaned with anguish. "He's dead. My Canada goose. It's Charlie. See the band on his leg?"

"I'm so sorry, . . . so sorry. She never did this before. I wouldn't have brought her . . ." Cassie was too miserable to finish. She wished she and Midnight were home, that this terrible thing hadn't happened.

She'd known her pet was a retriever, but—wait—retrievers don't usually kill. Cassie hopefully suggested, "Maybe she just picked it up. Perhaps it was already dead."

Mrs. Jordan gave her a blank stare and went into the trailer. Sheila, scowling, leaned against a tree. Cassie fought back tears and sat down beside the dead goose. Midnight whined, crawled from under the trailer on her belly, and dragged herself into Cassie's lap. Cassie hugged her.

"It's okay, Middie. You didn't know better. We'll go home next weekend," she said. Then she remembered her vow not to go home. Besides, she couldn't believe Midnight had killed that goose.

3 A Sad Trip to the Woods

The next few minutes stretched and pulled at Cassie's mind like a taut rubber band. Her fingers stroked the dog's coat. She couldn't think what to do.

She still felt numb when Mrs. Jordan startled her: "Here's a garbage bag to put it in." The ugly green plastic snapped in front of Cassie.

Mrs. Jordan instructed Sheila, "Take Charlie to Mr. McLaughlin, and see if he'll take care of him. I can't stand to bury him. Anyway, we don't have a shovel."

Cassie didn't want to touch the bird, but Midnight was her dog, and she felt responsible. She picked up the goose and placed it in the bag. Before pulling the drawstring, she lifted the banded leg and looked at it. The lettering was worn and faded. She dropped the leg and pulled the bag shut.

Sheila had gone to the car and yanked the dog's chain from under the seat. She linked it around a large oak. Cassie snapped the other end of the chain to Midnight's collar.

Cassie picked up the bag that held the goose. She

followed Sheila, who left the trailer site, subdued and quiet. Gravel grated under their feet.

"Mr. McLaughlin lives over there." Sheila pointed to the roof of a house behind some evergreens in the distance.

Cassie moved up beside Sheila. Behind them, she heard Midnight whine and bark. Cassie wished her dog would be as quiet as she was at home in their apartment, but here everything was new and exciting. She was glad the Jordan's trailer was on the island where the dog's barking wouldn't disturb other campers. Cassie wished she could think of a way to keep Mrs. Jordan from hearing her. Midnight would eventually accept being on the chain, but it might take a long time.

"I've never been to Mr. McLaughlin's house, but I know it's up that path." Sheila waved to the right. "He's a great big friendly man. When he stripped coal off this land, he didn't just cover the hole when he was done. He made it deeper and turned it into two lakes. The back lake filters out the water before it gets to the front lake. That's what makes the front lake so beautiful."

They followed a path that left the gravel road and wound through a clump of evergreens. Abruptly, they came into sunlight almost at the front door of a rambling stone house. Sheila knocked and Mr. McLaughlin appeared at the door.

"Mr. McLaughlin, we have a goose—," Sheila began.

Cassie interrupted, "I'm so sorry. My dog may have killed your goose. I don't think she did, but she dragged it to the trailer in her mouth. I shouldn't have brought her to Sun Lake. I had no idea—"

Sheila broke in, "Will you bury it?"

"Wait," Mr. McLaughlin commanded, holding up his hand. He questioned them until the whole story was told. Then he assured them, "There's no need to apologize. It's a wild Canada goose. It doesn't belong to me. Of course, I try to protect them, but this isn't your fault. You didn't try to kill the goose."

Cassie wished he'd say he knew Midnight hadn't killed the goose, but he didn't. His blue eyes were sad but kind. He grabbed a shovel from his tool shed, and they followed him into the forest.

She apologized again while Mr. McLaughlin dug a hole to bury it. Then she watched him lay the body of the goose into the hole and press in the stiff legs.

Cassie had always imagined that death, even the death of a goose, would be dramatic. But burying Charlie seemed like planting onions in Grandma's garden in the spring. Plop, plop. A few shovels of earth covered it. The dead goose was gone, over and done. Cassie was relieved.

They said good-byes to Mr. McLaughlin at his house. Instead of heading toward the trailer, Sheila turned the opposite direction.

"Where are we going?" Cassie wondered.

"To the phone booth."

"Who are you calling?"

From her pocket Sheila pulled a scrap of paper and unrolled it to read a phone number. "Someone."

"Oh, no! You're up to something again."

Sheila guarded her secret behind a smirk. At the

phone booth, she left the door open while she dialed. Cassie heard her say, "Sheila Jordan, Sun Lake Campground."

Oh, no! She was giving the address of the campground. Suddenly Cassie remembered the last time Sheila had given her address on the phone. A carton of blank cassette tapes had arrived, along with a bill. They had had to send them back, and the postage was four dollars.

"No, Sheila!" Cassie pulled at her sleeve.

Sheila hung up with a grin on her face. "It's free!"

"That's what you said about the tapes," protested Cassie.

"But this is different."

"What is different?"

Cassie tried to pin her down with her eyes.

Sheila squirmed, then used a deliberately casual voice: "Just a packet of information about wildlife. A toll-free number I found in the newspaper. Don't worry. There's nothing to pay."

Cassie wasn't convinced. Sheila's "nothings" usually turned out to be "somethings." All the way back to the trailer, Cassie tried to wheedle Sheila into saying what she ordered. At last Sheila settled the matter, "If you don't know, how can anyone blame you this time?"

Right! Cassie thought. She dropped the subject.

At the trailer, they poured sodas, then unhooked Midnight for a walk on the leash. When they returned to their campsite, Cassie grumbled, "Every time your mom looks at Midnight, she'll remember Charlie, so maybe we should stay away."

"Just this afternoon, until Mom gets over it," Sheila agreed.

They wandered around until six o'clock. Then she and Sheila raided the refrigerator, made sandwiches, and ate outside. Late that evening, Mrs. Jordan found them and apologized for her anger. By bedtime, she was nearly her cheerful self again. She insisted that Cassie bring Midnight in, to sleep by her bed as she did at home.

Later, the lights were out and the dog and Sheila were both breathing deeply. Cassie lay on the top bunk listening to the night sounds coming through the tiny trailer vent by her head. A baby cried at a distance. A dog barked. Suddenly, there was a heavy thudding sound on the roof above her head, followed by a metallic clatter she recognized as lawn chairs falling over on the concrete slab outside the trailer.

Cassie's heart began to pound. *What was that sound on the roof? What made the chairs fall?* She suddenly felt alone and afraid. She had never slept in a forest before. The prayer she had prayed when she got into bed now seemed completely inadequate, so she added some more: *Dear God, I'm afraid. Keep me safe.*

Trust me, came the answer. Cassie lay very still. Her mind went into the forest, seeing teeming life in the soil, the air, the ground, in every stump and tree. Moving life of every size and shape. Drowsily, she rolled over and slept.

4 A Bit of Dry Paper

"Cassie, wake up. . . . *Cassie, wake up!* . . . **Cassie, wake up!**"

The whisper grew louder. Cassie opened her eyes. A shadowy nose loomed in the faint light, inches from hers. She flinched, then focused on the face—Sheila's face. Memory returned. She was in the overhead bunk of the Jordans' trailer. Sheila, standing on the floor, faced her at eye level.

"Cassie, wake up. Let's go. Deer come early to drink. Be quiet. Don't wake Mom."

Cassie rubbed her eyes. "Give me a minute."

Sheila's face disappeared. Remembering the dead goose, Cassie wanted to melt into the bed and disappear. Yesterday she'd been sure her dog didn't do it. This morning she wasn't sure. Maybe Midnight *did* do it—not purposely, though.

Lovable, bouncy Midnight—so innocent, so proud of herself! She had only tried to please! As a retriever, she had simply obeyed her genes.

Cassie stared at the thin light coming through the

trailer's tiny vent window. Sitting up, she ran slim fingers through her thick curls, rubbed her eyes, and stretched. She'd better hurry. Sheila was nearly dressed.

A bird twittered. Thump, thump, thump went Midnight's tail against the floor. The thumping stopped abruptly. A low growl came from the dog's throat. Her nose pointed toward the door. Cassie suddenly remembered the sounds she'd heard before falling asleep. She would ask Sheila later. Right now, Sheila was impatiently waiting for her.

"Hush, Middie," whispered Cassie sternly, remembering how Midnight had barked at chipmunks in Rock Creek Park. The dog whined softly.

Cassie stretched and threw the blanket back. Sliding her feet over the side, she dropped silently to the floor, pulled on her jeans with "knee bumps" from wearing them the day before, and yanked on a knit pullover.

"Ready," she whispered.

Sheila, shoes in one hand, unlatched the door. She warned once more, "Shhh!" and pushed on the door. A thin slice of light entered. Suddenly, Midnight threw her weight against the door and hurtled through. There was a clatter as the dog landed on a folded lawn chair on the ground, scrambled up, and was gone.

Cassie gasped. Just in time, she remembered not to yell. They tiptoed outside. Midnight was circling, nose to the ground. She sniffed her way to the road and was gone.

"Oh, no! I forgot the leash!"

Cassie fumbled back inside and found the leash

and chain. Before she could reach the door, Sheila thrust her head inside, listened, and whispered, "I don't think Mom woke up. Sh!"

Cassie stepped out, and Sheila drew the door shut after her.

"Did Middie come back?" asked Cassie.

"Not yet. Look, we must have had a big wind in the night." Sheila set up the lawn chair beside the others.

"No," Cassie muttered. "Something knocked it over."

"How do you know?" Sheila's whisper was demanding.

Cassie, bent over, was pulling on her shoes. She would tell Sheila as soon as she found Midnight. Now she picked up a scrap of paper at her feet and put it in her pocket as she did at home. Mom said if everyone picked up a piece of trash instead of dropping one, there would be no litter. But *now* she had to find Midnight.

"Sheila, I have to call her. She may kill another goose."

"Don't call her. Mom might hear. Wait till we're away from the trailer."

They set off along the gravel road.

"Is she sure it was Charlie?" Cassie was remembering the dead goose.

"She who? Mom? Sure, she knows Charlie. Mom knows all the geese. She's painted most of them—all except some of the younger ones. When you're an artist, you notice details. Hey! Here comes Midnight."

Unabashed, Midnight trotted up and thrust her nose into Cassie's hand. Cassie nabbed her collar and let out a big sigh of relief. Immediately, Midnight tugged at her leash, pulling Cassie forward. Walking headlong, they soon had crossed the bridge and were on the mainland. At last, Midnight eased up and began sniffing along the grass beside the road. Cassie had time to look around her.

Feathery wisps of fog hung over the water. Wild roses, clambering over the rail fence, scented the air. Cassie stopped to sniff a rose, and Midnight ran around her, wrapping Cassie in the chain. The dog's tail, damp from dew, lashed against Cassie's leg as she untangled herself.

"No chance of seeing deer with Middie along." Sheila seemed glum.

Her remark cut Cassie. Her dog seemed to be bothering everyone. She couldn't think of anything to say, so she just walked on. The cool dampness seeped through her clothes. She shivered and jammed her hands in her pockets. In the right pocket was the paper she'd picked up as they left the trailer.

She scanned the road ahead for a trash can. *No trash cans!* she thought with surprise. In Washington—but this wasn't Washington. Mom had a fit if she found paper in pockets of clothes to be washed. Paper shredded or wadded into balls in the wash machine.

Mom would say—Cassie stopped the thought and giggled. Her good humor returned. "You know," she told Sheila, "Mom's not here, but I hear her talk in my head, 'Cassie, pick up paper, put it in the trash, don't get your shoes wet, stay out of the grass,' and on and on. I even listen to her. See, I picked this up at the trailer." She showed the paper from her pocket.

"Wait!" she cried. Cassie stopped abruptly and stared at the paper. "I picked up this gum wrapper right in front of the trailer a few minutes ago, and it's bone-dry!"

"What about it?" asked Sheila.

"This is spooky." Cassie paused, thoughtful.

"What's spooky?"

"Do you chew Wild-Nut gum?"

"Of course not, Mophead. I have braces on my teeth. I can't chew gum. Why'd you ask?"

"Look around. Do you see anything dry? No, there's heavy dew over everything. But this paper is fresh and dry!"

"Let me see." Sheila reached for the paper. "That means . . ."

"That means someone dropped it right before we came out," finished Cassie. "And that means someone was snooping around the trailer. Why would anyone do that? And another strange thing happened. That chair didn't just fall. After you were asleep, something thumped on the trailer roof, and then the chair fell. Maybe someone stood on the chair, tried to get to the roof, and then fell. Doesn't this wrapper prove someone was there this morning?"

"I don't know. But you're right—that wrapper's crisp and new. Sure seems funny to me. We won't say anything to Mom about this, right? She was upset enough about the goose."

"Right!" agreed Cassie. "Mr. McLaughlin—the man who buried the goose—would he be walking around late at night or early in the morning? Does he chew gum?"

Sheila laughed. "How should I know? Mr. McLaughlin? He owns the place. He could be walking around any time he wanted. Maybe—oh, I don't know."

"What? What don't you know?"

"I was going to say, maybe Mr. McLaughlin was checking to see if we had tied Midnight, and maybe he dropped the wrapper. But Mr. McLaughlin wouldn't throw down paper on his own campground. Of course, it may have blown out of his hand. . . ."

"But there's no wind," Cassie observed.

Sheila's long legs set a fast pace. Cassie skipped now and then to keep up. Her mind was racing. Somehow, she couldn't believe Midnight had killed the goose. If not, how had the goose died? And who was at the trailer last night? Or this morning?

Cassie's feet moved automatically as her mind puzzled over the gum wrapper.

5 Midnight Hides

Cassie was following Sheila when, ahead of them, a motor coughed, started up, and broke into the morning quiet. Sheila turned around and waited for Cassie to catch up.

"Must be Lyle," Sheila assured Cassie.

"Lyle?" Midnight barked and surged forward. Cassie leaned backward and tugged on the chain.

"Yes, Lyle. Don't you remember? I told you! He cuts the grass."

In another hundred feet, the fence turned a corner and ran behind a grassy alcove. In the center was a large picnic pavilion. At the back of the alcove, Cassie saw the source of the noise. A weed cutter hung from the bare shoulder of a man, who guided it along the fence row. Midnight strained toward him.

Sheila tiptoed on the dewy grass. Cassie allowed Midnight to pull her after Sheila. When they reached the man, Sheila shouted. He turned and shut off the motor.

"Sheila, you're back!" He was grinning.

Cassie saw he was young, sixteen or seventeen, she guessed. His muscles rippled under bronze skin. His eyes were brown, a darker brown than Cassie's, and his hair was straight and almost black.

Sheila tossed her wheat-blond hair. "Cassie, this is Lyle."

"Hi, Lyle," Cassie responded.

"Cassie's with us for the summer while her mom goes to school." Then Sheila demanded, "Lyle, why are you cutting weeds so early?"

"I have a college class at nine o'clock. When I get back, it's too hot to cut weeds. Weeds don't mind if they're cut wet, and this is my machine, so I run it when I please."

"College! You aren't old enough for college!" Sheila's blue eyes were incredulous.

"The community college lets us take courses as soon as we've finished our junior year in high school." Lyle leaned against the fence and looked toward the newcomer. "Well, Cassie, how do you like Sun Lake?"

Cassie hesitated then said, "I like Sun Lake. It's beautiful, . . . but my dog killed a goose and—well, I shouldn't have brought her."

Lyle's eyes seemed to turn even blacker. He stared at her, then looked toward the mountain peak as he quizzed her. "Did you see your dog kill it?"

"No-o-o," admitted Cassie. "But she brought it in her mouth, and it was dead, and its neck seemed broken."

"Well, you might be wrong. Maybe she just found it."

That thought cheered Cassie. "I can't believe she

did it. Really, I can't. She doesn't even catch chipmunks in Rock Creek Park. Mom says she's all bark and no bite."

Cassie, eager for more convincing words from Lyle, searched his face. He turned his head away. His profile looked—arrogant. No, not arrogant. Distant. She was disappointed as she realized that he had gone away from her into his own thoughts.

Sheila didn't seem to notice the change in him. She spoke in a bubbly voice: "Lyle, who would be out walking around the campground late last night or early this morning? We have to know because we found—"

Cassie didn't let her finish. She jerked Sheila's arm and muttered in her ear, "Don't say it!"

Aloud, Cassie said, "We didn't leave a note to tell your mom where we went. She might be worrying about us. Nice meeting you, Lyle. Good-bye." She pulled Sheila onto the road.

"Why'd you do that?" Sheila blue eyes flashed.

Cassie walked fast, putting distance between herself and Lyle. Sheila followed, grabbed her arm, and repeated, "Why'd you do that? You were rude."

"Lyle could have dropped the gum wrapper. He was out early, and I think he was chewing gum. Didn't you see his mouth moving? Why would he be snooping around the trailer?"

"You think Lyle was outside our trailer? Nah. So what if he was? He wouldn't hurt a fly."

Behind them, the weed cutter sputtered, then droned on.

"Don't be so sure," Cassie cautioned her. "There's

something different about him. He's—"

"Indian. Native American." Sheila supplied the words. "I know that. His name—all of it—is Lyle Sawyer Littlefoot. Anything wrong with that?"

"No, but his face looked . . . stormy."

They had reached the porch of the deserted camp store. Sheila flopped down on an outdoor bench. "Stormy—what kind of look is that? His eyes are always black."

Cassie tried to put into words what she felt. "He knows something. He's hiding something."

"That's silly," Sheila stated with finality. Before Cassie could say more, she jogged away. Midnight yapped and lunged eagerly after Sheila until the chain pulled the dog up short, nearly upsetting Cassie. Giving in, Cassie broke into a jog after Sheila.

They had come half circle around the lake. Cassie could see the island across the water to her right. As they jogged along the breast of the lake, the sun rose above the hills. The water shattered into millions of dancing chips of light. Swimming toward them, steadily, effortlessly, came a flock of geese in close formation.

"They're *beau-ti-ful!*" Cassie stopped to admire them. "Wait!" she called, but Sheila jogged on. Reluctantly, Cassie followed, passing the geese.

Abruptly, Midnight changed direction. She barked at the geese and jerked the chain backward, pulling Cassie around. Before Cassie could recover, the dog bounded down the bank to the water, pulling Cassie after her.

Cassie's feet slid on the wet grass. She lost her balance and came to rest at the water's edge. Her clothes were soaked. The hand she had used to break her fall was sticky.

Geese waddled onto the bank, unafraid. Midnight ripped the leash from Cassie's hands.

The dog rushed at the geese. She barked and grabbed at them with her mouth. Cassie watched in consternation. A gander came after the dog, hissing, neck forward, wings pumping. As the wings flailed, the blunt beak found its mark for a fierce pinch. Yelping with pain, feathers flying about her, Midnight retreated for refuge behind Cassie. The big goose followed, and the strong pinions of its wings slashed across Cassie's face.

Cassie jumped to her feet and ran up the bank to the road. Midnight stayed close, cowering beside her. The gander turned back, honking. The other geese began pecking about on the ground, waddling away as they fed.

Cassie viewed her hands with disgust. In one palm was a large glob of goose droppings. She tried to look around one hip to inspect the back of her jeans. Unable to see, she felt with her clean hand, and it came away covered with feathers and droppings.

"Look at you!" Sheila hooted. She had returned and was laughing so hard she bent over with her head between her legs. "You're a mess! You have doo-doo on your hands and doo-doo on your pants and doo-doo on your face and feathers in your hair!"

Cassie wanted to hit her. Instead, she moved away, then stumbled over Midnight. She touched down with one hand on the ground, and regained her balance. Sheila was still laughing.

"Shut up!" Cassie yelled. "SHUT UP! We'll go back to Washington with your dad on Sunday. Then you won't laugh at me. You won't have to worry about Midnight and dead geese."

"If you go home, you're either homesick or you're a quitter," Sheila shouted back.

"I'm not!"

"You are!" Sheila's face was red.

Cassie screamed back, "Anyway, Midnight didn't do it. She doesn't kill animals."

"Well, if you're so sure she didn't do it, find out who did! Don't quit and go home."

A voice echoed in Cassie's head. What was it Sheila had said on the way? That Cassie would go home in three days? She couldn't let her words come true.

"I won't! Just to spite you, I *won't* go home!" Cassie declared.

Suddenly, she felt ridiculous. She knew she looked funny with droppings and feathers smeared over her. She began giggling. Sheila laughed again. They laughed together until they were weak.

"I didn't know geese could be that fierce," gasped Cassie at last.

"Here in the mountains, they'd say the gander gave Midnight a flopping. You were in the way, Mophead, so you got flopped, too."

Cassie thought Sheila sounded like Job's comforters, but she knew her friend cared. She wiped her hands on a patch of clean grass. They headed home for breakfast.

6 Joseph the Storyteller

Thursday passed quickly. Sheila was eager to introduce Cassie to her friends, so the girls walked to the Dari-Treat. When they arrived, Sheila was disappointed to find none of her friends there. She asked about them but was told, "Only Ace works here anymore, and he doesn't come in for this shift."

On Friday afternoon, Sheila's father arrived. Bill Jordan was also escaping from the Washington heat. He would be coming to camp as many weekends as he could. On Saturday, he worked all day painting the roof of the trailer.

"I'll get my maintenance work out of the way," said Bill. "Then I can enjoy the weekends."

Cassie and Sheila passed frosty glasses of lemonade to the roof and ran errands for him. When Sheila complained about helping, Cassie blurted out, "I wish *my* dad were home so I could help him."

She saw Sheila look at her and suddenly wished she'd kept quiet. Missing her dad was bad enough, but having Sheila pity her was worse. What had Sheila said about her in the car? Had she called her a shadow, or was she talking about a cougar?

Next morning at breakfast, Mrs. Jordan announced, "Today is Sunday. We go to the pavilion for worship services, Cassie. You don't need to dress up."

"You'll like Joseph's stories," Sheila assured her. "He doesn't preach. Time goes fast when Joseph talks. It's lots better than church at home."

Mrs. Jordan smiled at Cassie. "Your mom said you go to church at home."

"Almost every Sunday." Cassie suddenly wished she were home with Mom, walking up the steps of First Community Church. She was sure Mom would say a prayer for her. That thought brought a warm feeling that chased away the longing for home.

"Of course, I'm coming with you," Cassie agreed.

Cassie and Sheila walked behind Bill and Mrs. Jordan to the pavilion at 10:00 o'clock. When they were almost to the picnic shelter, the lively notes of fiddles reached them.

"That's Joseph and his wife playing the fiddles," explained Mrs. Jordan. "Their music brings the campers in."

The four of them found a seat at one of the tables under the roof. Sheila continued to whisper to Cassie, who tried to be quiet. Cassie, interested in this new experience, counted the people—about fifty. The music stopped. "Now join us in singing," invited the man named Joseph.

When the hymns were finished, Joseph stood up to speak. Sheila whispered, "Sometimes you wouldn't believe his stories are even in the Bible, but if you look them up, they're right there. Other times, he tells his stories as they would be if they happened today."

Cassie tried to shut out Sheila's chatter. Joseph was saying, "You're out here in the forest." He waved his arm toward the trees across the lake. "You sit down on a rock. Everything is peaceful around you. You say a prayer of thanks to God for all this beauty. Then, while your mind is tuned to God, you have a vision. A vision is like a wide-awake dream. You can even talk in a vision.

"In your vision, the tree branches above you are swept back, the sky opens, and a canvas sheet, held up by the corners, comes down to earth. You hurry over to see what's in it, and you're amazed to see that the sheet is full of animals. There are cows and horses and chickens and dogs and cats. There are bears and foxes and cougars and geese and raccoons and skunks. All kinds of animals!

"Now the voice of God comes out of the sky. He says to you, 'Kill any of these animals and eat them.' But you protest, 'Any of them? Lord, I couldn't eat the skunk or the cougar or the cat or the dog. They aren't fit to eat.' "

Joseph's voice stopped. Cassie thought of eating a skunk and nearly gagged. Joseph stood quietly waiting. A bird sang in the stillness. No one moved. At last he resumed his story: "The sheet full of animals disappears. You're still wondering about this strange vision when the sheet comes down again. Three times in all, the sheet full of animals comes down. Three times, God's voice says, 'Kill and eat.' You say, 'Well, I'll eat the cow, but not the skunk. It's not fit to eat.'

"God's voice answers you, 'If I say these animals are fit to eat, then you must not call them unfit!' And God reminds you, 'After all, I made them. Don't insult me, their Creator. It is you who thinks them unfit, but unfitness is in your mind, not in the animal.' "

There was silence as Joseph paused again. A chipmunk scurried between the feet of the silent listeners. Eventually Joseph continued, "What a strange vision you've had! God once gave a man named Peter a vision similar to this. Listen while I read from the Bible, Acts, chapter 10."

Cassie had heard the story before, but it had seemed like a fable. Sitting here by the lake, talking about animals by name, the story seemed real. *Fit animals and unfit animals? Midnight? Geese? Cougars! Cats?* In her mind she saw the black cat on the cover of the book in the bookstore. What was the name of the book? She couldn't remember.

Her mind had wandered, and she missed part of the Scripture reading. She began to listen to Joseph again. ' "But God has shown me that I should not call anyone common or unclean.' "

Cassie suddenly recognized a face behind Joseph. Lyle Littlefoot was leaning against the stone wall of the fireplace at the end of the pavilion. *What was there about Lyle that made him seem so interesting?* she wondered. Was it the way the light sifted across his face?

She squinted to see him better. *He's chewing gum again!* Cassie punched Sheila with her elbow and whispered, "Lyle's chewing gum!"

After a moment, Sheila breathed back, "You're right!"

The rest of the service passed by quickly. Cassie couldn't keep her eyes off Lyle. She saw him turn and leave. Then, for a brief time, Joseph caught her attention again. He concluded his story, "The animals in this Bible story stand for humans. The animals in my story represent humans, too. But today, I want you to think of *all* the inhabitants of earth: plants and animals, men and women. We must all learn to live together, respecting, supporting, and loving each other.

"Animals were created as well as human beings. Yes, we can destroy whole species of animals. But if we do, we make ourselves poor. Yes, we can ignore whole families of people, those of a different race or nationality or country. We can sit back and let others destroy a family of people. But we make ourselves poor if we do that. God cares about what he has created, and that's an example for us. Each species and each person has a purpose for being here on this planet.

"What should we do about those who are being killed? I don't know. I honestly don't know. I'm not even sure God will give all of us the same answer when we ask. Do you teach each of your own children in exactly the same way? No. I wouldn't want to predict what God will ask of you."

Again, Joseph stood quietly, as though lost in thought. Cassie thought, *What an actor this man is! His silences are as important as his words.* Then she changed her mind. *No, he's speaking from his heart without trying to impress anyone at all. The best actor is not an actor!*

Suddenly, Joseph smiled. "Enough talk about the world! You're here to rest and recover inner peace. Look around you! The lake, the sky, the forest—a feast of beauty! Today, this moment, let's enjoy and treasure the wonderful variety of plants, animals, and people around us."

Joseph began to sing softly,

O Lord, my God, when I in awesome wonder
Consider all the worlds thy hands have made . . .

The campers joined Joseph in singing. When the last echoes of "How great thou art, How great thou art!" drifted back to them, Joseph held out his arm and softly pronounced a blessing, "Go in peace."

There was an awkward silence after his words, then the campers began talking and moving around. Cassie looked for Lyle, but he was gone. Sheila urged, "Come on, Cassie. Let's go to the camp store for Dad's newspaper. I always get it for him on Sundays."

Sheila turned to her father and held out her hand. "Da-ad?"

Bill grinned and dropped a dollar bill into her hand.

A second time, Sheila begged, "Da-ad?" Her hand was still out.

Bill scrounged in his pocket and brought up another dollar bill. He dropped this one in her hand, too. "What's this world coming to? The tip is now more than the paper!"

Sheila giggled. "Come, Cassie."

As they turned to leave, Bill added, "Get something to fend off starvation. Chicken barbecue's not till 2:00."

7 In Search of a Stranger

The next days passed quickly. Cassie and Sheila walked every morning, but saw no deer, only geese.

"There were about seventy geese last summer," Sheila recalled one morning. "They seem to be disappearing."

"Let's count them," Cassie suggested.

That wasn't easy to do because the geese were swimming around. Sheila tallied sixty. Cassie found fifty-eight. They compromised, telling Mrs. Jordan there were only fifty-nine this year.

The next day a bitter wind come up. Cassie was amazed that the end of June could be so cold. In D.C., smog bound everything in flannel once summer began. Cassie complained that it was too cold to sunbathe, but Sheila coaxed until Cassie got into her bathing suit. By the time they reached the water, they were both shivering. After a miserable hour on the beach, they returned to the trailer.

The following day was warmer, but still cool. Sheila wanted to lie in the sun near the camp store so she'd see when the mail arrived. She wanted to nab the package she'd ordered by phone before her mother saw it. Cassie was irritated that Sheila still wouldn't tell what she ordered. On the second day of their sunning beside the camp store, the package arrived.

Cassie read the return address over Sheila's shoulder: Wildlife Hot Line, Baltimore. Inside were flyers and booklets, but no demand for payment. Cassie breathed deeply with relief.

Sheila handed a booklet to Cassie. It was filled with maps of the eastern states, one map for each endangered animal. In each state was printed the number of the animals of that kind reported in the state that year.

Cassie stopped paging to read the map for panthers: "Virginia, 69; Pennsylvania, 67; West Virginia, 50; Maryland, 29! Can you believe this? That many people called in and reported seeing panthers, but panthers can't be caught to prove they exist! Most states have made killing one illegal. Now that's strange. If officials really believe there aren't any, why do they say you can't kill one?"

"Don't ask me," Sheila fended off her question. "You're as smart as I am."

"No, I'm—" Cassie's mouth was open while she searched for words. "Well, I don't feel like I am," she murmured.

On the way back to the trailer, they counted geese again—fifty-eight this time, they agreed. But the geese were on the grass and darting here and there for food, so they couldn't be sure of the count.

Later that day, they hid the pack of wildlife information under the mattress of Sheila's bed. "Just in case," Sheila commented. "We might need information. Since I'm going to be a wildlife biologist, I'm starting now."

"Why are we hiding this?" asked Cassie.

"Well . . ." Sheila looked uncomfortable. "Mom will tease. This way, it'll be easier if I change my mind."

The next morning when they walked, they checked the geese again—fifty-six. More geese missing! What could be happening to them?

"Bad for the geese, but good for us!" declared Cassie. "The killer can't be Midnight. She's been tied up since the day the goose flopped her."

Late that afternoon, they were on the back side of the lake, returning home, when they saw a strange man. Near the causeway, an old logging lane trailed upward toward the dark forest on the mountainside. It was marked with a sign, "To Fossil Rocks."

A man came down this track just before they reached it. He turned toward the camping grove, nodding quickly as he passed. A camera was strapped around his neck, and under his arm was an enormous folded-up thing which Cassie guessed was a tripod. His lightweight jacket bulged at the pockets. Mud streaked his face and army camouflage clothes, and he wore thick-lensed glasses under a khaki safari hat.

When Cassie saw him, Midnight retreated to her side, growling. Midnight's hair stood on end.

"Weird!" muttered Sheila, shaking her head and turning to watch him go out of sight. "In the morning, let's find his campsite. We'll check out this strange character. Maybe he chews gum."

Cassie's pulse quickened. "Yes, let's investigate

him! I'd feel better doing something, even if it turns out to be nothing."

After breakfast the next day, they tied up Midnight so she couldn't follow them. All morning they searched for the stranger among the wooded campsites. Finally, after lunch, they saw his safari hat at site 32.

The man under the hat was reading a book while he ate at his picnic table. Beside him, a surly shepherd dog sat up and growled at them. Before they had a chance to retreat, the man glanced up, saw them, shut his book, and disappeared into his camper.

"He acts like he doesn't want us to notice him. What'll we do now?" asked Cassie.

"Go to the Dari-Treat," proposed Sheila, glumly.

"We've been there five times already, and none of your friends were around," Cassie pointed out.

"Maybe this time . . ." Sheila's sentence faded away.

They were soon walking in single file along the county road, Sheila in the lead. Sheila tried to talk to Cassie, but the wind seemed to blow the words away. She heard Sheila say, "Ace . . . shift change."

Cassie tried to walk closer. Head down, she kept her eyes on Sheila's heels to avoid stepping on them.

Cassie wore her jeans again, to be like her friend. Sheila insisted on wearing jeans because she thought her legs were still white. Cassie was annoyed. She didn't like her own legs—her knees were knobby—but that didn't keep her from wearing shorts and skirts. Still, she was Sheila's guest, so she humored her.

Now, walking along the road, a thought popped in

her head: *We're always like this: Sheila first, me second.* Her toes caught Sheila's shoe and stripped it off her heel.

Sheila stopped, bent down, and pulled on her shoe. Zip, zip—a string of cars passed.

Cassie cupped her hands around her mouth and shouted, "What did you say?"

". . . and maybe Ace will be there."

"Where?"

"Where we're going, Mophead! The Dari-Treat."

Zip, zip, zip. More cars passed. With one hand Cassie shielded her eyes from the blowing grit. Sheila had called her Mophead again! Why hadn't she just called her Dummy? That's what she meant. Cassie could tell by her voice. She squelched an angry flare-up and wished she'd told Sheila she didn't want to come along.

Cassie's feet hurt. She groaned. Cassie seemed to have walked more miles since coming to camp than she had walked in a year. She was stiff and sore from all the walking. Back home, Sheila was a cheerleader. Cassie realized that her own favorite activity, watching TV, had not prepared her to keep up with Sheila at camp. In fact, she hadn't even thought of Sheila as active until they came to Sun Lake, or of herself as a rag doll by comparison.

Now, as she walked, Cassie thought about the mud on the stranger's clothes. Something had seemed peculiar about the mud. That's it! It was dark, still damp. Where had he been, so near, to get wet and muddy? She eyed the gray soil beside the road. Was it dry? She two-stepped sideways and scuffed her shoe into the

48

ground. A puff of gray powder dusted her ankle.

Sheila was shouting once more. After a garbled sentence or two, Cassie heard, "Adopt-a-Grandparent . . . sent meals to old people."

Cassie strained her lungs to yell back, "Who sent meals?"

"The lady who owns the Dari-Treat."

"What about her?"

"I said she belonged . . . sent food . . . didn't cook for themselves . . . fixed a meal every day . . . delivered it."

"Who delivered it?"

"Ace or Karen or Bill."

"Oh. . . . " Talking was too difficult. Cassie gave up. She refused to answer Sheila's next shout.

The forest on each side of the road soon gave way to an overgrown meadow, then to the parking lot of the Dari-Treat, deserted except for several cars at the rear.

8 An Old Friend and an Old Baby

They ordered cones. Then Sheila asked the waitress, "Is Ace here?"

"Who?"

Sheila turned away and griped to Cassie. "There's no one here that I know." Her voice showed disappointment.

"Oh, yeah?" boomed a voice behind them. The girls whirled around.

"Ace!" Sheila's face lit up. "I didn't know you. You must be six feet tall. And your voice. . . ."

The grinning boy had the widest freckled face Cassie had ever seen. Freckled arms and blue-jeaned legs protruded from an enormous white apron.

"This summer I cook and take out garbage and deliver meals," Ace said. "In half an hour, my shift is done. On my way home, I take a meal to Old Grouse. Want to go along? I'll drop you off at the camp."

"Oh, Ace! You have your driver's license! I'm absolutely envious!" Sheila's blue eyes sparkled. Cassie thought she looked pretty any time a boy talked to her.

Her face seemed to come alive. Cassie wished her own brown eyes would light up like Sheila's.

"Got my license three days ago!" Ace glowed. "Who's your friend?"

"Oh, sorry! Ace, this is Cassie," Sheila responded. "She's staying with us this summer. Cassie, this is Ace."

"Hello, Cassie. Now, Sheila, I've got to finish my shift. Are you going along to Old Grouse's?"

"Sure, but who's Old Grouse?" asked Sheila.

"Sure!" Cassie's voice echoed Sheila's.

Ace chuckled. "Old Grouse is the man I take dinner to. Named him that 'cause he's always grousing—complaining. And he brags how he can still shoot grouse. Grouse are like pheasants. They're gone in a whir and hard to shoot. Don't see how he could hit a barn door, shaky as he is, let alone a grouse. But he's a grouchy old fella, so I don't question him."

Ace twisted the garbage bag shut. "Soon be done. Don't leave." He headed for the rear of the building.

Outside at a table, Cassie waited with Sheila for Ace. She rotated her cone slowly, letting her tongue run around the cold sweetness in careful spirals. How hot she was!

Sheila, opposite her at the table, finished her cone, lay down on the wooden bench, and tugged at her jeans to bare her legs to the sun.

Cassie sighed. If she had Sheila's long silky blonde hair and her clear blue eyes with their fringe of dark blonde lashes, she wouldn't worry about her legs. Her own brown lashes, even long and curly, didn't hold a candle to the special blonde of Sheila's. Besides, she had discovered she didn't like sunning with Sheila—Sheila became a grunting mannequin in the sun.

An abandoned newspaper wilted over the edge of the table. Cassie pulled it close and read a headline, "Sixteenth Case of Rabies Reported This Year."

"Sheila, do geese get rabies?"

"Dunno," muttered Sheila.

"How would a rabid goose act?"

"Dunno," grunted the form on the bench.

In the silence that followed, Cassie wondered, *What if the dead goose was rabid? What if Midnight's rabies shot is no longer effective? What if my dog never had her shot after all?* Her eyes traveled down the page and halted at a small heading, "Man Claims Mountain Lion Exists."

"Sheila! Look—"

"Ready to go?" Ace's voice boomed behind her. Cassie jumped, and Sheila shot to her feet.

Ace carried a large, take-out container. "Old Grouse's food," he stated. He led the way to the back of the parking lot.

"Where are Karen and Bill?" asked Sheila.

"Got other jobs," explained Ace.

He paused by a car painted multishades of blue, unlike any car Cassie had ever seen. On the waves that curled down the sides were painted the words OLD BABY. He patted the hood and announced, "This is it, girls!"

"What *is* this thing?" Sheila expressed what Cassie was thinking.

Ace grinned. "Old Baby." He looked proud. "Fixed it up from two old cars. Paid a hundred dollars for 'em both. Had to buy a few things at the junkyard. And I used some putty—lots of body putty—and paint. Got leftover paint from the body shop. A work of art, isn't it! Worked on it all last winter. Get in. It won't bite."

"Probably drown us!" Sheila giggled.

Ace opened the front door and made a mocking bow to Sheila—which set her giggling again. When she was settled inside, he handed her the container of food to hold. Ace opened the back door for Cassie, and she slid in, feeling irritated that Sheila was in front with Ace. Just once, she wished Sheila would be second. Then she was annoyed at herself for being so petty. Sheila didn't really try to be first. She *was* first.

Ace got in, the doors slammed shut, and he zipped into traffic and headed toward the camp.

9 Old Grouse Tells a Tale

The tick of turn signals alerted Cassie that Ace was turning off, down a drive that was a narrow slot between scrubby meadow and state forest.

"Old Grouse lives down this lane," he said. "Wouldn't think there's a house in here, would you?" He opened his window and thrust his head out to see the road.

Tall grass swished against the car on both sides as he eased over ruts and rocks. At last, they came to a clearing at the end of the road. A rotting yard fence surrounded an old house, long since free of paint.

Overgrown shrubs and ancient, wind-broken trees shaded the house. Its windows sagged like old eyes in a wrinkled face. A rusty lawn mower was shoved under the rickety porch. Behind the house, the state forest was dark with thick ropes of wild grapevines.

An old, gray-whiskered man appeared in the doorway. He pushed the screen door open. Five dogs slunk out, growling, murder in their eyes.

"She-e-e-t up!" strained the old man's voice. He

waved a cane at the dogs. They obeyed and disappeared under the house.

"Ku-um in," he quavered.

"Come along," Ace told the girls. "I always stay while he eats. He's a crank, but he's lonesome."

Sheila got out and Cassie followed. Ace strode ahead. Before they reached the porch, their feet crushed hundreds of springy, little trees.

Old Grouse swung his cane in the air. "Dumb dogs," he griped. "Feed 'em and they'd still bite you if they had half a chance." He led the way into the kitchen.

The house smelled of dank, rotting linoleum, dogs, and food, all mixed with wood smoke. In addition, when Cassie got near the old man, she smelled a strong body odor. His skin was gray. She wondered if the gray would wash off.

A cast-iron cookstove nearly filled the kitchen. From the teakettle on top rose a geyser of steam. Old Grouse took a metal handle, hooked a round plate in the stove top, lifted it, and peered in, then settled it back with a clank.

He hung up the tool and turned to them. "It's a little warm in here. Cain't shake this cough. Had pneumonia last year. Doc says I got to keep warm or they'll put me six feet under within a year. Cain't smoke no more neither."

Cassie found herself saying in her mind: *Cain't— rhymes with paint, the way he says it.*

The old man pulled out chairs and waved for them to sit down. She gingerly sat on the edge of one so she wouldn't break through the frayed reed seat.

Ace introduced Sheila and Cassie. He set the packaged dinner on the oilcloth-covered table and brought a knife, fork, and spoon from a drawer.

"Mighty nice to have you ladies visit," Old Grouse said politely. "Pity ya didn't come sooner. I git tired a-bein' alone." He attacked his food, stabbing the roast beef and waving it about with a two-tined fork."

"Well, what's the news, boy?" he quizzed Ace.

"Nothin' much," replied Ace.

The old man complained, "Every day this boy says, 'Nothin' much.' He works out there where people just leave them newspapers layin' round. D'ya think he'll tell me the news? Na, he won't. It gripes me no end. And it ain't no use I buy one. Eyes're bad and I cain't read noway."

"I don't have time to read it myself," Ace responded. "Cassie was reading the paper. Ask her."

"I just read about sixteen cases of rabies this summer," Cassie volunteered. "And a man claiming mountain lions exist."

"Mountain lions!" The quavering voice grew loud and strong. "Hain't heard of them in years. I killt one oncet. Last day of deer season, and the gang was drivin' deer toward me, and I was a-standin' and a-waitin'."

His bloodshot eyes wavered. He began coughing. At last he went on. "I'd been waitin' a long time when I seen the laurel bushes shakin'. Figured there was a buck in there. I sighted my gun, but no head appeared. I waited. Then I seen him, crouchin' along like cats do, with his belly low to the ground.

"Well, I got scared 'cause I couldn't see nothin' that

he could be creepin' up on 'cept me. So I sighted him in and pulled the trigger. That cougar rolled right over and died. Always wisht I'da got him mounted, 'cause nobody'd believe me."

"I thought you were talking about a mountain lion," Ace objected.

"Mountain lion, cougar, panther, puma—don't matter—all the same. Around here folks call the black ones panthers. But the one I killt was a regular tan one. Left it to rot in the woods. That was long ago. Ain't legal to hunt 'em now. Cain't hunt, cain't smoke."

His voice caught and he began coughing. Still coughing, he stood up and bent his head down. At last, with a horrendous clearing of his throat, he went outside and spat from the end of the porch. Cassie nearly gagged. Ace was watching her with amusement in his eyes, so she laughed instead. If Ace could find it funny, she could too.

The old man returned and sank into his chair. "Boy, go get me my chawin' gum off that shelf above the sink. Gotta have something to kill my cravin'."

Ace crossed the room to the sink. His hands searched the shelf. He glanced down. As he brought the gum to the old man, he commented, "I thought you couldn't hunt anymore. What are those things in the sink?"

"A mess a squirrels." The voice took on a crafty whine. "You wouldn't begrudge me a mess a squirrels, would you? I got 'em soakin' in salt water to take the wild out."

Sheila jumped up. "I want to see," she said. Cassie followed her to the sink. The scrawny pink forms of two skinned squirrels floated in water in a pan.

A chair scraped behind them, and Old Grouse appeared at the sink. "Have some gum," he offered. He held out sticks of Wild-Nut for Sheila and Cassie before putting it back on the shelf. Sheila's and Cassie's eyes met. Wild-Nut! Cassie pulled off the wrapper and put it in her jeans pocket. She knew she had a match for it back at the trailer.

"Where did you shoot those squirrels?" Cassie asked.

"Outa the hickory tree." The old man hobbled to the table and sank into his chair.

Ace looked at the girls and declared, "Time to go. Good-bye, Gramps."

As they left, Old Grouse called after them, "You never bring me enough gravy. More gravy next time, boy."

They got into the car. As the doors slammed shut, Cassie exclaimed, "I didn't think people still had stoves like that! Old Grouse is different from anybody I ever knew!"

"He's different all right!" Ace agreed.

Cassie settled back in the seat. She thought of the story Joseph had told. Which animal in the sheet would stand for Old Grouse?

"A possum!" she muttered aloud.

"What did you say?" asked Sheila.

"Old Grouse reminds me of a possum. He acts more dead than he is. And he's definitely unclean. Remember Joseph's story?" Cassie giggled.

"Yes!" agreed Sheila.

Cassie didn't say more. She was thinking of the

Scripture Joseph had read: *Never think of anyone as inferior.* Cassie had agreed with him. Now she caught herself feeling superior to Old Grouse. She felt upset as she faced her own prejudice.

10 Librarian from Painter's Hollow

Eat, walk, sleep, and sunbathe: that's all we've done for three days, Cassie thought. At ten o'clock in the morning, she was lying beside Sheila in the sun.

Sheila had a blister on her heel, and her burned skin shed long, fragile strips, but she wouldn't give up walking or sunbathing. She wore rubber flip-flops on her feet and sunbathed before the sun got high in the sky. *Stubborn—that's what she is,* thought Cassie.

Ouch! Cassie swatted a stinging fly. If only something would happen. Anything! Well, not quite anything! Mom said people had to make things happen—like Mom getting her degree. Mom knew what she wanted. *What do I want?* wondered Cassie.

Her summer was slipping away. She wished Ace would come by. A boy friend would help—not a boyfriend, but a friend who was a boy. The summer wouldn't be wasted if she could practice talking to boys—but other girls did that without having to practice. Then again, other girls had brothers or at least lots of friends to practice on.

Beep! Beep! Cassie's eyes flew open and she sat up. Maybe Ace—no!

Mrs. Jordan rolled down the car window. "Want to go along to the library?" she called. "I quit painting. I can't concentrate today."

Sheila propped her head up and moaned, "Not me!"

"I want to come along!" Cassie yelled back.

"Well, hop in. I'll take you to the trailer to change. Sheila, please get out of the sun. You're burned. You'll have skin cancer by the time you're twenty."

"Mom!" Sheila wailed. "I'm not tan enough. . . ."

Cassie slammed the car door shut, then hopped back out to call to Sheila, "Bring my beach bag when you come up."

Mrs. Jordan waited in the car while Cassie changed. Midnight, tied to a tree, barked as they left.

Fifteen minutes later, they were at the library in the small town. A short, bustling lady with graying blonde hair hurried forward. Her face was softly wrinkled into smile lines.

"Mrs. Jordan!" she exclaimed, showing her pleasure. The two women hugged.

"Cassie is part of our family this summer," Mrs. Jordan introduced her. Turning to Cassie, she added, "And Mrs. Williams can always find what you need."

"Thank you!" Mrs. Williams looked a little flustered from Mrs. Jordan's praise. "What can I do for you today?"

"I want a good mystery and an art book as usual," stated Mrs. Jordan. "What do you want, Cassie?"

Cassie flushed. "Any—" She started to say "anything," then thought that would make her sound as though she didn't have a mind of her own. She said, "Something. Something about Canada geese."

"Here, this is the wildlife section, and here's a book about how geese talk."

The librarian left her.

Geese talk! Cassie opened the book and read, "Geese communicate by pumping their necks up and down when they feel threatened and are about to attack. Keep your distance until the displays stop."

She remembered the morning she'd been "flopped," as Sheila called it. Once painful to think about, the memory now made her smile. She read on, discovering that Canada geese make many motions to communicate, and the motions are called displays.

She lay the goose book aside. She would take it. What else should she take? Maybe a book for Sheila. Or a book about mountain lions? She glanced at the clock. She would have to hurry. Mrs. Jordan might be ready soon. Her eyes skimmed the shelves. Here . . . the words stood out and flagged her: *Wild Cats: Grosset All-Color Guide.* Quickly she took it from the shelf. Now *this* would interest Sheila.

Cassie checked out the two books she had selected. Mrs. Williams smiled when she saw the book about cats. "If you're interested in cats, there's a good article in an old issue of *Discover.* Would you like to read it? You can check it out if you'd like."

Before Cassie could nod yes, Mrs. Williams buzzed off to find the magazine. When she returned, she handed it to Cassie. The glowing life-sized eyes of a cougar stared at her from the cover. Its whiskered muzzle filled the bottom half of the page.

Mrs. Williams confided in a soft tone, "They're all wrong, you know. This article says there are only fifty Florida panthers left, and all other eastern panthers are extinct. Those scientists believe that, but I know better. Out there in Painter's Hollow where I was born—" Her hand waved and Cassie's eyes followed the wave, half expecting to see a tumbledown house built against the side of a ravine. But dull library-wall plaster faced her.

Mrs. Williams was still speaking. *"Painters*—that's what the old mountain people called panthers. People today see the sign, Painter's Road, and think the road was named for a house painter or a sign painter, but it wasn't. It was named for panthers. The road goes over the top of the mountain where there are rocks as big as a living room. That's where the painter's dens were— panther's dens. Anyway, down in Painter's Hollow, we heard them squalling at night. Every once in a while, one would come down, and we'd see it outside."

"You really saw a mountain lion?" Cassie asked.

"Yes, five of them in the time I lived in Painter's Hollow. I was just a little girl, but I remember. Now all that land is in the state forest and as wild as ever. You can't tell me mountain lions are extinct. Nothing has changed there at all. Here . . ."

She riffled through the magazine and found the article. "They're wrong, but the rest of the story is good—how they study Florida panthers. Someday they'll be studying panthers here, too. Well, enjoy yourself reading. If I find more on big cats, shall I save it for you?"

"Oh, sure," Cassie agreed. She took her books and

magazine outdoors to read until Mrs. Jordan was ready to go. She had only a few minutes to wait, time enough to look at the pictures and skim the article in the magazine.

Sheila will love this, she thought—the article featured a female biologist. She closed the magazine. Out there, in the blue hazy mountains, were panthers—painters—in Painter's Hollow, waiting for Sheila, the biologist, to discover them. Sheila, the biologist! Biologists knew better than to burn their skin in the sun.

Sheila, a biologist! But—what will I be? The question, a new-blown bubble, grew and grew and burst with nothing inside. She blinked her eyes. Tears blurred the mountain. At least Sheila wanted to be *something*. Cassie hadn't the slightest idea what she wanted to be. Was something wrong with her?

She jumped when Mrs. Jordan said, "Ready to go?" right beside her.

As they drove home, Cassie looked into the vine-tangled dimness of the forest beside the road. She imagined that high in one of those trees a mountain lion crouched.

He's stretched flat on the limb and his long tail twitches and his eyes are glowing and he watches . . . watches. . . . Cassie shivered. *If trees had eyes, they would know if there are mountain lions here. Why did God make mountain lions, anyway?*

They drove under the stone arch: SUN LAKE! Ahead of her, the sun danced on the blue water.

11 The Muddy Man Makes a Date

"I've been here three weeks and it seems like three months," Cassie had just written to her mother. She added, "Mrs. Jordan is painting, and Sheila is sunbathing beside me on the beach. Her skin is so red, I'm surprised she doesn't worry about getting skin cancer."

She sighed and reread the sentences for the tenth time. If only she'd told her mom about Midnight and the goose when it happened. Telling her now would be like pulling on a snag in a knit sweater—more and more would unravel!

Today was too lovely to be writing anyway: cotton-ball clouds in a blue sky, sailboats on the water, children's laughter, and a gentle breeze that ruffled the lacy trees and tickled her skin.

Cassie sighed again. The letter with its three sentences was smudged. She held it to her nose. Yes, it smelled like suntan lotion. Her eyes hurt. She squinted, and the words dissolved into dancing black spots. Cassie shut her eyes, and white blobs appeared where the paper had been. She daydreamed.

Sun Lake seemed to have become part of herself. Mom had become a distant memory. The water was real. The lake's owner, Mr. McLaughlin, and Lyle Littlefoot, who tended the grounds, were real. Ace and his car, Old Baby; Mrs. Jordan with her bouncing hair and paintings drying in the shed—they were real. Joseph, the storyteller, was real. Old Grouse was real.

Sheila, especially Sheila, was real, like the sister Cassie never had. She was often at odds with Sheila, but wasn't that how sisters were anyway? Even Mr. Jordan, Sheila's father, seemed more real than Mom. He had come last weekend and gone again. For a moment, Cassie allowed herself to long for home.

Then she smiled. She was pleased that she was keeping her promise to herself. In spite of her dog and the geese, she hadn't run home to Mom. Sheila's prediction that she'd go back to D.C. homesick would not come true.

"Cassie, will you put some lotion on my back?" Sheila rolled over on the blanket. Cassie squeezed a glob of white cream on her friend's lobster-red back and rubbed it in lightly, knowing her fingers could roll up burned skin at the slightest pressure. Sheila was too sore to be in the sun, but she wouldn't listen to Cassie or her mother, except to use sunscreen lotion. At least her sunburn settled the jeans problem. Sheila couldn't wear jeans now!

Cassie put white blobs of lotion on each of her own legs and rubbed them in. She stretched out on the blanket, then lifted her head to look down across her body. After three weeks of walking, her waist was smaller and her legs firmer. Three weeks of sun had darkened her skin to the color of overdone toast and stamped the shape of her bathing suit on her body. For the first time since she'd known Sheila, she wasn't envious.

Cassie sat up once more to check her dog. Yes, Midnight dozed lazily under a small tree where she was tied. The dog was getting accustomed to being tied outside and no longer fought the chain, although Cassie knew she'd be off in a flash if she got loose even for a second.

She lay down and let her mind wander. How hot it must be in Washington now. Her mom would drag herself home from school exhausted. Again, Cassie wished she were home. Then she pulled her mind to the present, determined not to be homesick. In a minute, she fell asleep.

Cassie was awakened by the honk-honking of geese. She sat up and found herself surrounded by them. The flock, together as usual, had found Mrs. Jordan, who had brought along a bag of bread crumbs. Cassie sat still, trying to remain a part of the landscape. Midnight, a wiser dog than she'd been early that summer, ignored the geese, too.

Geese! She could simply tell Mom, "I'm sitting in a flock of geese, fifty-six of them." Or was it fifty-five? Not that it mattered. She wrote the sentence quickly lest she forget it.

"Ouch!" A goose pecked her toe. The geese, startled, fanned away.

Cassie glanced at Mrs. Jordan, who was drawing furiously. By now, Cassie knew how she worked, sketching the geese when they came close and painting in background when they were absent. Mrs. Jordan didn't paint copies; each picture was different.

Mrs. Jordan stopped abruptly. "The geese seem to be dwindling. I just *know* there were more when we came. And I'm sure there were more last summer."

"Fifty-five or fifty-six," Cassie reported. "We counted them one day."

Mrs. Jordan was chewing on the end of the pencil. Her long red-gold curls, tied up with a scarf, bobbed up and down. "Are you sure? I counted only fifty-one just now."

"The rest are probably somewhere else," Cassie suggested.

"Well, I hope so," muttered Mrs. Jordan, "but geese usually stay together."

The geese were moving on, honking as they went. Cassie lay down and shut her eyes.

She was nearly asleep when Midnight began a frenzied barking. Cassie sat up. Her pet was barking at a large dog accompanying a man who was talking to Mrs. Jordan. He was—yes, he was the stranger with the muddy face and the camera who had come down the road from Fossil Rocks, the one camped in site 32.

His shepherd dog sauntered toward Midnight and stopped about a yard out of Midnight's range. Midnight threw herself toward the dog, coming up against the leash and falling back again and again. The shepherd stared at Midnight, seeming to wonder what the ear-piercing yipping was about.

"Cassie, please get Midnight quiet," called Mrs. Jordan.

"Samba, come!" ordered the man.

The shepherd turned away from Midnight with a superior air, returned to her owner, and sat down.

Cassie unhooked Midnight's leash. "Quiet, Middie," she soothed the dog, then led her back to the blanket. Midnight quieted and sat down. Before Cassie could stop her, she licked Sheila's face.

"Keep that dumb dog out of my face," Sheila shrieked. She flailed her arms about and sat up. Her face was beet-red.

"Sheila, we have company." Mrs. Jordan's voice was cheerful but determined. "This is Mr. Armstrong, a writer. He'd like to write a feature for the *Washington Post* about our family vacations and my painting. What do you say? Should we let him do it?"

Sheila stood on the blanket, looking confused and not quite awake.

"I'll come back later," offered Mr. Armstrong. "Discuss it among yourselves."

"Good," Mrs. Jordan responded. "We'll let you know soon."

"Mom, let him do it," Sheila suddenly begged.

Cassie smiled to herself. She might have known Sheila would jump at the chance to have her picture in the paper. Cassie could see the headlines now, "Beautiful daughter vacations with mother."

Mrs. Jordan was seeking her attention. "Cassie, do you agree? You're part of our family this summer."

Cassie hesitated. For a moment she felt disloyal to her own family, to Mom in Washington and Dad in New Jersey. Then she smiled. How silly! Mom and Dad would understand. Choosing felt good!

"I'd like to be in it," she declared.

"Then it's settled," stated Mrs. Jordan. "We'll do it."

"I'll need to interview you," explained the man.

"Could you drop by for dinner Friday night? My husband, Bill, will be coming for the weekend. He'll be here then. We'll get to know each other, since we're neighbors here. About six?"

"Fine. Six o'clock then. Come, Samba."

As he turned to leave, Cassie suddenly remembered how suspicious he'd looked in his muddy clothes. She quickly noted, *No hat today, dark hair and tanned, medium height, glasses with thick lenses, trim build, knit pullover and walking shorts, clean white tennis shoes.* He could be any D.C. executive on vacation. Not memorable, except when he smeared mud on his face. *Smeared mud!*

She realized, with a start, that her subconscious had collected impressions and made a deduction without her awareness. *He smeared mud on his own face!*

She stared after him. Yes, a man who dressed as neatly as Mr. Armstrong would not go around with mud on his face unless he wanted it there. He must have had a purpose for doing that. But what purpose?

12 Dinner at Six

Sheila's dad, Bill, arrived from Washington about five o'clock on Friday night. He immediately started the grill. Sheila and Cassie carried steaks and steak sauce, barbecue tools, salt, pepper—anything Mr. Jordan needed—from trailer to picnic table.

Mr. Armstrong came at six, carrying a large flashlight and his camera. Samba was at his heels. She began to growl when Midnight, tied to a tree, ran up to her. A stern command from her master quieted Samba immediately. She ignored Midnight's sniffing by holding her nose high and refusing to touch noses.

"I'm William Jordan." Sheila's dad offered his hand. "Call me Bill. I hate being called mister. I hear that every day at the office. William is even worse—sounds like a real stuffed shirt!" He chuckled.

"Don Armstrong," returned the man.

"Our daughter, Sheila, and our daughter for the summer, Cassie." Bill waved them forward. The girls shook hands.

Mrs. Jordan came outside. "Call me Peggy." She

smiled and extended her hand in welcome to Mr. Armstrong.

Cassie was always surprised to hear the name *Peggy*. Sheila called her mother Mom, and the kids at school called her Mrs. Jordan. On her artwork, Mrs. Jordan signed, "Marguerite Jordan." Only Bill called her Peggy.

At Mr. Armstrong's command, Samba lay down. Midnight lay, too, her nose to Samba's nose. There she stayed the rest of the evening, refusing to leave Samba's side. Only her eyes rolled as she followed the action around the fire. Cassie laughed at her and spoke to her, but still the dog refused to lift her head.

After dinner, Mr. Armstrong asked to see Mrs. Jordan's finished canvases. Next, he photographed the family. By the time he got out a notebook to interview them, daylight was fading. Bill put several logs on the fire to provide light for Mr. Armstrong's writing.

Mr. Armstrong began the questioning. "How long have you been taking painting vacations?" he asked Mrs. Jordan.

"Since Sheila was about six years old. Let's see. Nearly ten years now." Mrs. Armstrong looked at Sheila and smiled. Sheila grinned. Cassie quickly calculated. *Six and ten are sixteen. How pleased Sheila looks. Nearly sixteen! (I'm nearly fifteen.) How nice of Mrs. Jordan to compliment Sheila that way!*

Cassie suddenly felt homesick. Her birthday was in October. Mom would have a birthday party for her, and her friends from school would be there. She stared into the fire as a tear trickled down her cheek. The next ten minutes passed without Cassie being aware of what was said. She was absorbed in longing for home. She tried not to wipe her eyes or blow her nose. At last, she excused herself and went inside. In the bathroom, she cried—and coughed—so everyone would think she went inside because of the coughing. She was glad it was dark when she went back out, so no one would notice her red eyes.

Mr. Armstrong focused his attention on Cassie. "You're back. Good! You're the only one I haven't interviewed. Tell me, do you like having a dog at the lake?"

Cassie knew a lot about that subject. Soon they were all laughing and talking about Midnight.

The interview was finished and they were chatting comfortably when Samba suddenly stood up. She faced the darkness. Her hair stood on end, and a rumble started deep in her throat. Midnight arose and growled, too.

"Probably a skunk," Mr. Armstrong suggested. "One's been hanging around my camper." He dropped his notebook and pen on the ground as he abruptly stood up. Then he scrambled in the dark to pick them up. Hastily he turned on his flashlight, said good-bye, and left with Samba at his side.

"What's wrong with *him*?" Sheila asked, disgust creeping into her voice. "He acts like he's scared or something."

"Okay," said Bill. "It's pitch-in-and-help time!" The lid of the metal trash can rattled. The girls helped him clean up the garbage.

Soon, they were all inside and in bed. Cassie snuggled down, glad to be resting. She shut her eyes and listened to the tap-tap-tap of Midnight's nails on the floor.

"Lie down," she commanded the dog, sternly. By the glow of a night-light, she saw the dog look at her. Midnight made a small whining sound and paced as before.

Cassie tried to sleep. The dog continued to whine and pace the trailer. Cassie switched on a light and tried reading a book. She thought if she ignored Midnight, the dog would lie down, but she didn't. Again she switched off the light.

From the bottom bunk, Sheila grumbled, "Why did you have to bring that dog along anyway?"

Determined not to argue, Cassie said, more cheerfully than she felt, "I don't know."

Finally, she traded beds with Sheila so Midnight could lie at the foot of the bottom bunk with her. She was nearly asleep when Midnight whined and crawled up the bed to put her head on the pillow beside Cassie's. Cassie looked at the clock: 2:00 a.m. She turned her head so she wouldn't have to breathe doggy breath and fell asleep.

Thump! She woke up. There was that strange noise on the roof again. Drowsily, she wondered what it was. Then she slept soundly.

13 Who Lurks Outside?

Saturday morning, Cassie awoke to darkness and rain drumming on the metal roof. *Who shut the trailer vent?* she thought. Then she saw Midnight's head resting on her arm and remembered she had traded beds with Sheila.

Cassie shut her eyes and let her mind wander over Friday night's events. *Why had Samba growled? Had she seen something they couldn't? Why had Mr. Armstrong left in such a hurry, dropping things in his nervousness?* She dozed off without trying to answer herself.

Much later she awakened with a start and leaned out of bed to see the clock. Nine already! *Too rainy for walking. Good! Sheila's a fitness nut!* she thought. From the back bedroom came Bill's soft snores. Cassie rolled over and slept again.

The slamming door woke her. She heard Bill say, "I guess she'll bark when she's ready to come in."

Mmmm, coffee smells so good! And bacon, too! Cassie thought.

Bill's voice rumbled, "It's nearly noon! About time

you two sleepyheads get up! Roll out!"

The bed swayed above Cassie. Sheila's legs appeared. *Thump!* Her feet hit the floor and she ran for the bathroom, calling, "Come on, Cassie!"

Cassie sat up. She pulled the sheet loose, wrapped it around herself, and headed for the bathroom, too. As she passed the mirror on the hall closet door, she glanced at herself.

She noticed with surprise that the sun had burned copper highlights into the pile of dark curls on her head. Her eyes startled her, too. They looked enormous and dark in a face that had grown thinner. Cassie looked twice to reassure herself that the attractive reflection was really hers. Yes! She slipped in the bathroom door and shut it quickly when Sheila squealed.

By the time she and Sheila dressed, Bill had the second round of bacon and scrambled eggs ready for them. As the girls ate, he and Mrs. Jordan had second cups of coffee.

Bill announced, "Peggy and I are going out for the day—what's left of it! We have some shopping to do. Later we'll have dinner and see a play at The Barn before we come home."

"Oh, good!" Sheila replied. "Don't worry about a thing. We'll be in before dark and lock the trailer door."

Sheila washed dishes and Cassie dried them as the Jordans prepared to leave. Mrs. Jordan put up her umbrella and walked to the car. Bill roared, "Great day for ducks!" He jumped and ran, water spurting in fountains from each step. Behind him the door banged, unlatched. Cassie closed the door, stood at the window, and watched until the car was out of sight.

Five minutes later, Cassie heard Midnight's short bark. She opened the door and Midnight rushed in. The unmistakable stench of skunk filled the room. Cassie gasped and put her hand to her nose. The dog shook water everywhere, onto Cassie and Sheila, the sofa, and the chair.

"Oh, Middie!" wailed Cassie. "Now you've done it! What will we do with you?"

Midnight's tail wagged. She put up one paw, eager to be petted. Cassie, fearing another drenching, patted her. The awful smell filled the room and burned Cassie's eyes. She smelled her hand. *Phew!*

Sheila moaned and rocked back and forth on her knees on the sofa.

"Oh, no! Oh, no!" she wailed. "Mom will have a fit when she comes home. That dog will have to stay outside."

Cassie ignored Sheila's moans. She took Midnight in the bathroom, turned on the shower, and tried to wash her. The smell seemed to get even stronger!

She got the chain and snapped it on Midnight's collar. Cassie dashed through the rain and chained the dog to the picnic table. By the time she raced inside, she was soaked. She scrubbed her hands but could not entirely free them from the smell.

As Cassie changed her clothes, she winced at Midnight's pitiful barking and whining. Through the window, she saw the dog cowering under the picnic table, coming out in the rain to whimper now and then. Cassie was grateful that the rain was warm.

When Cassie returned, Sheila held her nose. "You stink, too."

Cassie heard, but her mind was with the dog. "I *hate* to hear her cry."

"Don't even think of bringing her back in," ordered Sheila, firmly.

"Okay, but I can hardly stand to hear her cry."

"Me, too, but she can't be inside. Mom would say, 'And that's final,' so try to forget her," declared Sheila.

"What can we do?" Cassie let out a long sigh.

"There's *nothing* to do here when it rains. Nothing!" griped Sheila.

"We can read," Cassie suggested.

Sheila scowled and began wandering from window to window. Cassie settled into the built-in sofa with her library books. She browsed through the book about geese before she opened the one about big cats.

Sheila turned the TV on briefly, then off again. "Wish we had more than two channels here."

"Me, too. At home, I'd love a day like this. Mom would make popcorn, and we'd both read."

Cassie focused her attention on the book. "Cougars are secretive animals," she read to herself. She reached out for the big pillow on which she usually rested her book and clutched at empty space, her fingers brushing cool, slick vinyl. Nothing there! She was suddenly homesick for the soft, old, rose-colored sofa at home.

"Cougars are secretive animals." Her eyes wandered to the window where a gray-green gloom wrapped around the trees. If this were Washington, she'd at least see street lights.

"Cougars are secretive animals," she read for the third time. She shut the book, stretched out and tried to sleep, but Sheila dragged at her arm and said, "Let's play Monopoly." They got out the game and began to play.

At four o'clock, the rain stopped, and they opened the windows to air out the trailer.

"We could get tomato juice at the camp store and give Middie a rubdown to take away the skunk smell," suggested Sheila.

"Let's do!" Cassie was eager to go outside— anywhere, and if tomato juice would help Middie's smell, she'd try it.

They were soon on the gravel road. A slowly approaching car made them walk to the side where the road had turned slippery. Mud stuck to their shoes in big clods, but Cassie was too happy to mind. The air was warm and clear. Blinding sun flashed off the water. Grass and leaves were a brilliant green.

Midnight danced ahead of them, her body flipping back and forth. When they passed the geese, she trotted up to them. They gabbled and strutted away.

The girls tied Midnight outside while they went into the store. They bought two cans of tomato juice. Outside, Lyle was standing by the soft-drink machine. Cassie called, "Hi, Lyle."

"Hi!" Then he nodded toward Sheila. "I met your dad and mom leaving this morning. Everything going okay?"

"Yes . . . no, do you smell Middie?" Sheila asked.

Lyle grinned. He finished a long drink from the can of soda before replying. "Smells to me like Midnight

79

met up with my friends."

"Your friends?"

"Cutest little family of skunks you ever saw. When they were little, they'd eat from my hand when the mama wasn't too close. What you got in that bag?"

"Tomato juice," answered Sheila. "They say it takes away skunk smell. . . . What did you do today, Lyle?"

Cassie felt Sheila move away from her, toward Lyle. Sheila would do it again—take over the conversation leaving Cassie feeling speechless. Cassie spoke up with the first thing that came to mind. "You know Mr. Armstrong, don't you? The muddy man?"

"The muddy man?" Then Lyle interrupted himself. "Oh, I forgot to tell you, Mr. McLaughlin shot a raccoon that attacked his screen door yesterday. He thinks it was rabid. You girls be careful. Don't go near animals like that."

They started back with Midnight at their heels. At the trailer, they tied her up, put the tomato juice in a small bucket, wet a washcloth with juice, and rubbed her down. The dog looked so funny trying to lick off the juice and not liking it that Sheila and Cassie laughed until their sides ached.

"Shall we wash it off now?" Cassie asked when they had used all the juice.

"Let it work for a while," decided Sheila.

They ate leftovers from the refrigerator while they waited. At dusk, they took warm soapy water outside and bathed the dog once more. When Midnight was rinsed and towel-dried, they put their things away and took the dog in the trailer. Sheila locked the door and pulled the drapes.

"I don't know if I'm used to the skunk smell or if the tomato juice really worked, but I don't smell skunk anymore," Cassie observed.

They returned to their Monopoly game. About ten o'clock, Midnight stood up. Her hair rose and her nose pointed toward the end of the trailer. A low growl grated deep in her throat. Cassie had never heard such a sound from her before. Fear shot through her, making her stomach contract. She stood up.

Sheila was walking toward the window when they heard a scream. It was the sound of a woman screaming, a piercing, keen, screeching sound that put terror in Cassie's bones. Sheila cried out and turned toward Cassie, grabbing her arm. They clung to each other for a moment.

Sheila whispered tensely, "It sounds like it's right outside! Let's look."

Sheila pulled the drapes open. Both girls screamed. The back of a man's head was so near the glass they could have touched it. He was gone in a flash, leaving them to doubt reality. Sheila dropped the curtain.

"Lyle! Lyle!" Both girls exclaimed. They looked at each other, questions in their eyes.

"Was that really Lyle?" Cassie wondered.

"I think so," declared Sheila.

The Jordans came home at 11:00. By then, the girls had agreed not to tell them about the scream. Sheila had said, "If we tell them, we won't get to stay alone for a long time." The girls faked sleep until pretense turned into the real thing.

14 To Fossil Rocks

"I'm having a great time, Mom," Cassie declared on the phone six days later. She pushed back brown curls sweated fast to her forehead. From the open door of the phone booth, she watched Ace trade the old banana-split sign for a slick, new one.

"You're not homesick, are you?" asked her mother.

"I was, a little, the afternoon it rained. But we've been so busy following—" She stopped abruptly. "So busy swimming."

Mom would worry if she knew they'd been following Lyle. Hurriedly she concluded her call.

The back of a man's head—the image haunted her. She and Sheila had spent hours talking about it. Had Lyle been there? Or was it a mirage, like an image of a pool of water, seen in the desert or over a hot road? During her next visit to the library, Cassie looked up *mirage* in the dictionary and the encyclopedia. She decided it was too dark that night for light rays to be bent or reflected into a mirage.

They had followed Lyle, looking for clues. Three

times on different days, he had gone toward Fossil Rocks, losing them in the forest. Fossil Rocks—what could be up there that attracted Lyle—and Mr. Armstrong? Today, she and Sheila had agreed to go to Fossil Rocks themselves.

Cassie found Sheila inside the camp store with Ace. "Cassie, it's settled," Sheila greeted her. "Tomorrow is Ace's day off, and he's going with us to Fossil Rocks. He's never been there either."

"Okay!" Cassie felt relieved. Three of them seemed safer than two in case they met Lyle or Mr. Armstrong or if—she shivered—*a panther followed them.* By the time they left the Dari-Treat, their plans were made.

The next morning, Cassie packed three cans of soda into a backpack while Sheila made sandwiches. Old Baby, its sides gleaming with wax, pulled into the campsite. Ace parked the car. Cassie quickly tied Midnight.

Ace had a big grin on his broad, freckled face.

"This way," called Sheila. Shrugging on her backpack, she led the way to Fossil Road.

"Are there really fossils up there?" Ace asked.

"I don't know," responded Sheila.

Ten minutes later, they paused at the bottom of Fossil Road. The mountain ahead of them had a wide band of deep green, almost black, above the lighter green of the trees they were entering. Its bald top appeared rocky.

Ace led up the road, which slowly dwindled into a trail overgrown with spindly, knee-high grass and wildflowers. Butterflies flitted in and out of patches of sun that leaked through the trees.

Suddenly Ace exclaimed, "Tire tracks!"

Sheila grunted as Ace stopped, and Cassie's chin thudded against Sheila's backpack.

"If I ne-e-ever return, you still have my hea-a-a-a-rt," crooned a voice.

Cassie looked around, confused.

Ace was pointing to two tracks of squashed grass. He laughed as Cassie looked for the sound. "That's my radio." He pulled it from his pocket.

A new song began, "Danger, danger, danger, danger, a-a-a-ah. You're in danger of my lo-o-ove."

Ace turned the volume low and put it back in his pocket. "Guess what happened at work yesterday? There was this lady who asked for a potato-chip sundae."

As Ace began his story, Sheila skipped ahead to listen and talk with him. Cassie followed.

Tire tracks, thought Cassie. Were they made by Lyle's old pickup or Mr. Armstrong's truck? If she had brought paper and pencil along, she could have sketched the pattern and checked it out.

The path grew narrower and steeper. They sat down to rest at the bottom of a steep ledge of layered rock. Above the ledge was the forest of green-black pines.

Cassie picked up a flat broken piece of rock. "Here's a fossil!" In the rock was a perfect fern pattern!

They hunted among the shale. Soon their pockets were full of fossil rocks.

"We could go home now," suggested Sheila.

"I'm going to the top," declared Ace.

"Me, too!" Cassie asserted.

She followed Ace. He was already halfway up the steep bank, bent over with his hands on the ground to keep from losing his balance. Sheila trailed behind.

In the pine forest, needles bounced under their feet. The trees became denser and darker. The trail was hard to see. Dead, dried, bottom branches and twigs snapped as they touched them.

Cassie shivered. "I don't like this woods. It's dark and spooky. Ooooh!" She brushed cobwebs from her face.

"Let's go back," groaned Sheila.

"I'm going on," Ace insisted. "It can't be much farther to the top."

Cassie stayed close behind him. After a time, the trees thinned out, it became lighter, and a few plants grew on the forest floor. Then a window of sunlight appeared, and at last, full sun. The peak was just ahead. They scrambled across a mass of rock to the top.

"Look! Sun Lake!" Cassie cried.

The lake glittered in the sun. To its right were two ribbons of highway. Beyond the lake, flecks of color identified the town where Cassie had gone with Mrs. Jordan to the library.

Beside her, Sheila drank in the view. "Whew! This [gasp] . . . sure is pretty, [gasp] . . . but I hate to go back through that woods."

"Me too!" agreed Cassie.

Ace was fumbling on the ground. "No fossils here," he reported, "just plain old rocks. Let's go down."

He started back at a fast pace. Cassie slipped and slid to keep up. Coming down, they passed through the dark pine forest quickly. Their pace slowed as they neared the rock ledge. They carefully inched to the bottom.

When they reached the wide path filled with wild-flowers and grass, Cassie suddenly remembered. "Hey, we forgot to eat. I'm hungry."

"Food!" Ace enthused. "I wondered what you had in that pack."

Cassie pulled off her backpack and plopped onto the grass. While she passed around sodas, Sheila took sandwiches from her pack.

"Roast beef," Ace approved. He popped open a can of soda, which fizzed over his hand.

"You really shook this one up, Cassie. It's warm, too!" remarked Ace.

"Well, you went so fast. What did you ex—" Cassie didn't finish the sentence because there was a sound of sliding shale from the rock ledge above them. She turned quickly and caught a fleeting impression of motion at the edge of the forest. But by the time her eyes focused on the ledge, everything was quiet.

"What was that?" Sheila asked.

"Dunno," mumbled Ace, his mouth full of sandwich.

"Maybe someone's following us," Sheila guessed.

Behind Ace's back, Cassie raised her eyebrows at Sheila, who ignored the hint and rattled on, "Rocks don't go sliding all by themselves. Someone must be up there."

"Or something. Maybe a bear," Ace added cheerfully.

"Stop that!" Sheila burst out. "I'm serious."

"I am, too. There are bears around here. The state stocked them a couple of years ago, and they multiplied. Now there are quite a few."

"Let's go," urged Cassie, standing up. She eyed the path ahead, eager to get back. As she set off down the trail, she heard Ace and Sheila following her.

When she rounded the next bend, she saw a man bent over beside the path ahead. Her heart leaped in her throat. Then he stood up, and she recognized Mr. McLaughlin.

"Mr. McLaughlin," she called out, glad to see him.

He waved back and waited for them to approach. At his feet was something. . . .

"What is it?" asked Cassie. "Feathers?"

"Some of our geese ended up here." Mr. McLaughlin pointed to bones and feathers at his feet. "Lyle just told me to take a look in the leaves beside the great oaks—the biggest oak of all is far back in that stand of trees." He pointed toward some enormous trees. Cassie could see that they had many branches coming from thick, tall trunks.

Ace began poking around in the leaves with a stick. Suddenly he whistled. "Here's a pile of bones, and they're not goose bones."

"Deer bones," determined Mr. McLaughlin as they clustered around.

He frowned. He picked up a long bone and looked at it intently. Cassie sensed he was keeping his thoughts to himself.

Ace continued to poke here and there. Suddenly he shouted, "More goose feathers!" They rushed over to look, but by the time they got there, he yelled from another spot, "Here's some, too!"

Mr. McLaughlin seemed to have lost interest in the feathers. "Think I'll take this deer bone back with me," he decided. He started down the path toward the campground, then turned back with a grim face. "Stick together, you three! Don't go wandering off alone."

They followed. When they reached the campground, Mr. McLaughlin was striding far ahead.

"Lyle must have been on the trail behind us if he found the bones and told Mr. McLaughlin," Sheila blurted out.

"Lyle? Who's Lyle?" asked Ace.

"He cuts the grass," Cassie explained.

"Oh, I know. He drives that old pickup with the fender falling off."

Cassie laughed. "You *would* notice what he drives!"

Sheila turned down the road past Mr. Armstrong's camper. "Let's see what Samba is doing. Dogs kill deer sometimes, don't they?"

They were still a distance from Mr. Armstrong's camper when the door opened and Mr. Armstrong came out.

Cassie jerked Ace's arm. "Shhh—" She stepped behind some bushes. Ace and Sheila followed her example.

Mr. Armstrong's face was streaked with mud. He popped a bucket into the bed of his truck and jumped in. The motor started, he backed out, and the truck was off down the road. There was no sign of Samba.

15 Night Sounds

A week later, Cassie woke in the night. She lay still, listening, her body tense. A noise had wakened her, but what? A dog barked in the distance. Samba? The bark was low and gruff like his.

Beside her, Midnight stirred, snorted, and settled back to a gentle snore. Cassie hoped her pet wouldn't be wakeful in the dark as she had been so often lately. The bottom bunk had permanently become Cassie's because she needed to calm Midnight when she began her restless pacing.

There! That sound again! It was a distant scream like the one they heard the night they saw "the head." They had fallen into the habit of talking about what they had seen when they pulled back the curtains as simply "the head," as though it had no body.

This time the scream was far away. There it was again, a chilling sound. Samba—surely it was Samba—kept up a growling bark.

She waited for the sound again. Her mind drifted to Ace. After their hike to Fossil Rocks, they had told him nearly everything—all but "the head." That seemed too unreal to repeat. If they told that, Ace might not believe the rest.

Where was Lyle anyway? They had not talked with him in a week. He seemed always to be behind them, keeping his distance, and he never caught up.

There! A rattling sound like a garbage can being dumped! Samba—and another dog—and another— now they were all barking. Then a snarling sound like two dogs fighting and, in a few minutes, silence.

Cassie was grateful Midnight didn't awaken. Poor dog! She was exhausted from chasing after Ace and Sheila and Cassie in the water yesterday. Dogs weren't allowed on the public beach, but Ace was a certified lifeguard, so Mrs. Jordan had let them swim from the island. They had had so much fun since Ace began dropping in after work almost every day.

Ace said Old Grouse was acting strangely. When Ace took his dinner early on Friday, the old man was cleaning his guns. Old Grouse said he wanted to be ready for rabid animals. That was understandable, to be ready for an emergency, but then Ace found the old man shooting outside with a rifle.

Ace had told Cassie sarcastically, "He's going to shoot some poor skunk with a rifle and blow him to smithereens."

Cassie had told Mom on the phone about Old Grouse—not about the guns, but about him living in the woods. She knew Mom couldn't imagine the way he lived. A few months ago, Cassie herself hadn't dreamed such a place existed just hours from the news center of the nation.

Up here at Sun Lake, she thought about geese and bear and deer and panthers—she couldn't forget Old Grouse's panther story. After all that, the nightly news on Mrs. Jordan's tiny portable TV seemed light and unimportant. They couldn't even snag a Washington station.

Finally, the night was quiet except for the distant drone of trucks on the highway. Cassie's mind drifted out of conscious thought. The next thing she heard was the sound of Sheila's whisper, "Cassie, wake up."

She opened her eyes. Faint light filtered into the room.

Cassie moaned. "Just once, can't you stay in bed like normal people?"

"Morning's the best time of the day." Sheila was exhuberant. "Besides we've been here a long time, and you haven't seen a deer yet."

"So I'll see one this morning?" Cassie knew her voice was sarcastic, but she was too sleepy to care. "I'm going back to sleep. Go without me." She rolled over and thumped her pillow into a comfortable shape.

"Okay, but you'll be sorry."

Cassie heard Sheila snap the leash on Midnight's collar. Sheila was taking the dog with her.

The door shut softly as Sheila went out. Cassie tried to sleep, but she wasn't drowsy anymore. At last she got up, dressed, and slipped out the door.

Which way had Sheila gone? Cassie set out in the usual direction. As soon as she was on the mainland, she paused. Around the bend ahead, geese gabbled. She walked stealthily, hoping to see them without being noticed.

A chipmunk scurried across the road. Cassie stopped and drew in a deep breath. The lake didn't smell like the ocean in New Jersey where Dad had once taken her. No, the odor was more like peat moss mingled with barnyard whiffs of manure and animals.

She rounded the curve. The geese—and deer! Two of them! A doe and fawn, its coat still faintly mottled, drank from the lake while geese gossiped all around them.

Cassie stood still and held her breath. The doe's head came up, alert and aware of Cassie's presence. Cassie's heart cried out to her not to be afraid.

The doe turned its head. The fawn nuzzled its mother, and the two of them moved on, their tan rumps flagged by white tails. The doe leaped the low rail fence so gracefully that she appeared to float, while the fawn scrambled through where rails were broken. Then the two of them flashed into the woods and were gone.

I've seen deer! Alone! Cassie wanted to rush off and tell Sheila, but not yet. She sat on a rock by the water to relive the memory of the beautiful animals. She thought, *I've been waiting for Sheila to show me the deer, but I saw them without Sheila. Why do I always expect Sheila to be the leader? I don't need a leader! I like being alone sometimes, too.*

She'd been sitting still, too deeply in thought to move. The geese had approached within several feet of her. A goose stretched out a long neck and pecked at her shoe. Cassie smiled as the flock surrounded her, their curiosity overcoming fear. There was Lila, Charlie's mate, wearing a legband. Others wore legbands, too. For a moment, Cassie thought about the scientists who banded geese to study them. She tried to imagine Sheila catching a goose! *No way!*

Cassie felt a rush of pleasure in recognizing Lila. She was gaining awareness of her new environment. Power! She couldn't quite put it into words, but it was something like power, this feeling she had for nature.

She watched a set of young geese swim after their mother while her mind drifted to Washington. Home! The summer was more than half over, and soon it would be time to go back. Would Mom understand the change in her?

Cassie thought of the paved streets and the early summer mornings when the sun came up shaded by a gray smog that hung overhead all day while the earth sweltered below. She'd never again be quite satisfied with city summers. But the spring and fall were wonderful in Washington—crisp, fresh sunshine and beautiful flowers. What was it like at the lake in spring and fall? Without leaves on the trees . . .

Her attention came back to the present as a goose gave another determined peck.

"Ouch!" She kicked toward the bold goose.

The geese scattered in alarm. Cassie laughed and stood up. When she stood still, they began to circle back almost immediately. She thought, *This is a good time to count them.* As they cautiously approached, she finished counting, "Forty-three, forty-four, forty-five, forty-six, forty-seven." That was all. Forty-seven and about ten goslings. She couldn't accurately count the young ones, so easily hidden behind the adults.

Forty-seven. What has happened to them? She

grew somber. Suddenly Cassie was aware that the sun hadn't quite topped the trees yet.

"Morning, Cassie."

She jumped in alarm at the voice right behind her.

"Good morning, Lyle," she responded, trying to keep her voice calm and even.

"Sure is beautiful this morning, isn't it?" His arm swept across their view of the lake.

"Yes! I just saw two deer. They're beautiful."

" 'No man or animal drinks above another at a lake.' " Lyle seemed to be quoting. Then he added, "I always think of that when I see the animals come to drink in the morning."

He looked at her intently. "You don't know what I'm talking about, do you? The brass plaque at the entrance to the campground says, 'No man or animal drinks above another at a lake.' "

"That reminds me of Joseph's story about the sheet full of animals," said Cassie. "No man drinks above another? What does that mean?"

"Well, streams run downhill, but the water in a lake is flat. Animals of all kinds drink side by side. The lake makes them all equal. Think about it."

"I'm not sure I understand. . . ."

"You will! Someday, you will!"

They stood now, watching the sky spread gold on the water. In the silence, Cassie remembered the missing geese. She tried to put her fear into words. "Something is happening to the geese. They're disappearing. And remember the feathers and bones up there?" She pointed toward the mountain. "What's going on?"

"Nature's beautiful, but it's cruel, too!" His voice

94

was so savage that Cassie looked at him quickly. His black eyes glittered.

"What do you mean?" Cassie spoke guardedly because Lyle seemed to be full of riddles today. She wanted to know more but was afraid of the anger she felt behind his words.

"We all eat each other," he added.

"No—animals do, but we—"

"Yes, we do. What will you have for breakfast?"

"Probably a pancake and saus— Oh, I see what you mean." Her voice trailed off as she thought about it.

"Well, as I see it, we're animals more than we think. We just don't want to admit it. And sometimes, one of us begins to kill for the sake of killing, not to survive."

Lyle's conversation was taking a frightening turn. Cassie decided to end it. "Look, I'd like to stay and talk, but I really must get back. Sheila will wonder where I am. 'Bye! See you around."

She was tempted to turn back, to take the shortest way home, but stopped herself with a stern mental reminder: *Don't be intimidated!* She headed on around the lake. Once she glanced back. Lyle was sitting on the rock where she had sat. He looked lonely, a tiny human not much bigger than the geese.

A short time later, she passed the stone with the bronze marker by the entrance. She stopped to read it: "No man or animal drinks above another at a lake." Yes, there were Lyle's words, under a heading, "Welcome to Sun Lake."

She turn and walked on, deep in thought. Yes, it was true. If she wanted to drink from the lake, she would have to stoop down as any animal might.

Human beings, with their pipes and pumps and water-purification projects, had created an image of superiority. Is that what Joseph meant?

As she rounded the last long curve on the lake, she stopped for a moment to look at a large round circle about fifty feet from shore. Sheila had told her long ago that it was a giant overflow pipe. Water spilled into it, making a perfect dark circle in the lake. Yes, the lake would be flat.

She puzzled over Lyle's words, "No man or animal drinks above another at a lake." Then once more she pondered Joseph's story of fit and unfit animals. Phrases from school entered her mind: "All are created equal . . . with liberty and justice for all." They were all related some way, but she couldn't yet say how.

As she headed for the trailer, her mind went back to Lyle sitting by the water. He had looked so lonely. How could he be dangerous? Then she remembered the anger in his eyes. *Be careful!* she warned herself.

As she neared the trailer, Cassie was glad to hear Sheila calling, "Ca-a-a-ssie. Ca-a-a-ssie."

"Coming," she answered. Midnight came bounding toward her.

16 Little Bo Peep

"Wish Ace didn't have to work this afternoon." Sheila's voice was a monotone that reminded Cassie of butter melted in the sun.

Without opening her eyes, Cassie said, "Me too!" She was almost asleep on her blanket in the shade. Cassie had come to the beach with Sheila, but she refused to make herself miserable by lying in the sun. These last days of July were sweltering and left her exhausted.

Cassie slid her fingers through her thick curls. Now she was wide awake and restless. She thought, *Here I am again, doing what Sheila wants!*

She sat up abruptly. "Sheila, I'm too hot. I'm going to the bathhouse for a cool shower." She headed to the camper for soap.

Yesterday, the hottest day of the summer, after all those dribble showers in the camper, Midnight had shown Cassie the showers in the bathhouse. Cassie laughed to think of it—Midnight running into the bathhouse, a lady screaming, Midnight rushing out with clothes in her mouth.

Cassie rescued the clothes and took them back. Midnight followed and scooted under the shower door. The lady had come flying out of the shower, screaming again, while Midnight stood under the shower with her head tilted upward, pleased at having found a way to cool off.

Yes, Midnight had shown her the showers. Cassie had taken Midnight to the camper, tied her up, and gone back to shower herself. How wonderful to wash her feet without banging her head into the wall as she did in the camper!

Now, with a fresh bar of soap from the camper, Cassie headed for the showers. Along the way, she noted Mr. Armstrong's camper. His truck was gone, and there was no sign of Samba.

Cassie showered slowly, letting the water cool her. She felt refreshed and happy. Humming to herself, she tucked her rolled-up towel under her arm and started back.

As she neared Mr. Armstrong's camper, she saw his truck parked there. Samba, tied up, didn't bark or seem to notice Cassie. What was wrong with the dog? Cassie cut through the trees as near as she dared.

Yes, something was different. Samba's ear was torn, and long scratches raked her back. The shepherd moved her head languidly, too sad to bark. "Samba, what happened to you?" asked Cassie softly.

"Stay away!" The shouted command came from the camper.

Cassie whirled around. Mr. Armstrong emerged, a threatening scowl on his face. Cassie hurried off, wondering what had made him angry.

She was too deep in thought to notice a man sitting on a picnic table. Cassie was nearly past him when the set of his head drew her attention. *Lyle Littlefoot!* She glanced back. He was following her!

Cassie slowed down as she considered what to do. She was tired of Lyle following her. Two elderly ladies in sweats and tennis shoes walked toward her. With people about, now was the time to confront him. She turned around to face him.

"Lyle, why are you following me?" Cassie called.

He stooped to tie his shoe, then stood and turned away.

"LYLE LITTLEFOOT!" she shouted toward his retreating back.

She ran after him and shouted once more, "LY-Y-LE!" She grabbed for his arm, her fingers brushing his sleeve.

Like a slow-motion dream, he reversed direction and pushed back his hat. "Hi, Cassie. What d'ya want?"

For a second, a smile filled out his cheeks. Cassie's eyes met his. His smile flickered and died. Facing him, the question stuck in her throat. "Why . . . why are—, " she stuttered but couldn't finish. Instead, she asked, "Did you see Mr. Armstrong's dog? Samba's all scratched up."

"Yeah, I know," replied Lyle. "Mr. Armstrong took her to the vet. That raccoon was rabid. It happened in the night, so the coon got away. I'm watching for it."

"Oh!" Cassie was relieved. "So that's what you're doing."

Lyle's eyes avoided hers. "Yeah, I'm watching for

rabid animals. I don't want one to attack you."

His answer surprised and pleased her. "Hey, thanks!" She was going to say more, but his averted eyes stopped her. *Wait a minute! He won't look at me,* she thought. *He's lying.*

"Be seein' ya," he said and strode off through the grass.

When Cassie got back to the camper, Sheila was already there and dressed. She agreed with Cassie's opinion about Lyle. "You're right. I know he's hiding something. Last summer he was friendly, but this summer he's getting spookier and spookier—like—he shows up at strange times and places and says strange things.

"The other day he even told me not to go walking alone in the morning. Why should it matter to him? I've a good mind to go out earlier and see what he's up to."

"Let's do!" Cassie agreed.

She and Sheila spent the rest of the day planning. With permission from Mrs. Jordan to sleep out, they settled for an empty picnic site between two occupied campsites.

"We'll be near people, just in case," Sheila observed.

They gathered plenty of wood, built a small fire in the stone fire ring, and rolled out their sleeping bags. Midnight, tied to a tree, could just reach them. They settled in, fully dressed as they'd agreed, even wearing their sneakers. Midnight promptly squeezed between Cassie and Sheila and lay down.

"Middie, you're a big baby," Sheila commented.

"I know she is." Cassie wriggled sideways to make room for her pet.

Midnight poked her nose under Cassie's sleeping bag and looked up, her black eyes soulful. Feeling sudden sympathy, Cassie patted her.

A tinny rattling noise brought Midnight's head up in alarm. Sheila and Cassie giggled. Sheila pulled the tiny travel alarm from her sleeping bag and rewound and set it. "I guess four o'clock will do," she declared with finality.

"Four o'clock! We've never gone out before six," Cassie protested.

"We want to be out by the gate when Lyle arrives. You know as well as I that he's always here at six. If we get up at four, surely we'll see him come."

"But it'll be dark at four."

"So? I've got a flashlight." Sheila pulled a long sportsman's light from under her pillow. "It's Dad's emergency light. I got it from the hold."

"The hold?"

"Yeah, that little door under the trailer where we keep the tools. Don't worry. I'll put it back."

"I'm going to sleep." Cassie rolled over and shut her eyes. Spying on Lyle had seemed so important earlier. Now it seemed pointless and silly and a little scary.

She opened her eyes long enough to be comforted by the lights in the camper window next to them. When a baby began to cry, she was grateful. She wanted to sleep so the night would be over as soon as possible.

"Sheep!" she muttered.

"Countin' sheep?" asked Sheila, giggling.

"Yeah," mumbled Cassie. It wasn't exactly true. She was disgusted at herself. Cassie knew she wouldn't be sleeping out if she hadn't followed Sheila. She was always following Sheila—following like a sheep. Sheila was Bo Peep, and Cassie was the sheep.

The cry of the baby in the camper was now a full-blown temper tantrum. Cassie let it lull her toward sleep. *Little Bo Peep has lost her sheep and can't tell where to find them.* The nursery rhyme hummed over and over in her head. She allowed her mind to unravel one connected thought after another until she slept.

17 Spying on Lyle

Cassie awoke in darkness when the alarm clattered. In the light from a few hot coals, glowing in the fire ring, she could see the cocoon shape of her sleeping friend. The cocoon twisted and split. Sheila muttered and fumbled and, at last, shut off the alarm.

Midnight stood up and stretched one black hind leg, then the other.

"Do it," said Cassie.

"Do what?"

"Put a piece of wood on the fire." Cassie was surprised at herself for giving Sheila a direct command. She was even more surprised when Sheila got up and carefully made an X of wood over the remaining embers, then shivered back into her sleeping bag. *Little Bo Peep has lost her sheep:* the silly nursery rhyme was still running in her head, hinting at something Cassie vaguely remembered.

"It's darker than I thought at four o'clock," Sheila muttered, "and I'm so sleepy. The baby kept crying, and the fire kept dying. I'd put on a log and crawl back in. Then I remembered Old Grouse's panther story and that library book you got me, and I couldn't sleep because I thought about panthers. And you! You snored! What a totally disgusting night!"

Cassie tried to get out of the sleeping bag, but her sneaker's rubber soles clung to the bag's flannel lining. Finally she sat on the ground with the bag around her feet. She gave a vigorous shake and emerged at last.

Cassie gripped Midnight's leash firmly in her hand. With Sheila flashing light on the road, they were off.

"Let's go to the stone arch," proposed Sheila. "Lyle will have to pass there. Luckily, there's only one way to enter this camp!"

At the arch, they sat on chunks of firewood with their backs against the mortared stone pillars. Midnight lay beside them and dozed. They waited. The sky washed out and grew pale. At last, a rosy glow painted the horizon. A car drove by, then another.

Sheila heard the clatter of Lyle's truck first. She pulled Cassie to her feet. "Come on!" she commanded.

They rushed behind the camp store just as the brown truck came into sight. Cassie held Midnight's jaws together so she couldn't bark. Lyle parked the truck and jumped out. He strode toward the water.

"He's getting a canoe!" Cassie whispered. She held Midnight's writhing body in a firm grip.

"He's unlocking the padlock on the chain," Sheila observed. "Now he's pushing off. . . . He's paddling away. Where can he be going at 5:30 in the morning?"

The canoe shrank in the distance. They stepped out and watched until it passed under the bridge to the back lake.

"Let's go!" urged Cassie.

They headed back, running and walking along the road to see where Lyle had gone. Soon they reached the bridge. From there, the canoe was a bobbing toy in the distance.

"Where did he go? The canoe's empty!" Dismay showed in Sheila's voice.

"Did he swim to shore?" asked Cassie.

"I don't know. He's not there . . . or could he be lying down in the canoe?"

"He has to be lying down. Why would he lie down?"

"We could rent a canoe to go and see," suggested Cassie hesitantly. She thought, *Here I am again, living in Sheila's shadow.* Sheila would have declared, "We *will* rent a canoe."

"We'll have to wait until the store opens. We can't unlock a boat like Lyle can," reminded Sheila. "Let's go eat breakfast. I'm hungry. We'll watch for him to come back."

Before they went in for breakfast, Cassie took one last long look at the tiny canoe, bobbing up and down on the water. Where could Lyle be? Did someone pick him up? Or—was he lying out of sight? If he *was* lying down, why?

She puzzled over the seemingly empty canoe as she ate Mrs. Jordan's blueberry muffins. She knew Sheila was thinking about Lyle, too, from the faraway look in her eyes.

Mrs. Jordan asked them how they liked sleeping out. Cassie said it was fine. Sheila nodded in agreement. Silence.

Mrs. Jordan gave an exasperated sigh. "You must not have slept at all, as sleepy as you two look," she commented.

"That's not it at all!" Sheila protested. "It's just that—"

Cassie hoped Sheila wasn't going to tell her mother about Lyle. She butted in, just in case, with the first question her mind popped up: "How deep is the back lake, anyway?"

"Deep enough to drown in," snapped Mrs. Jordan. "You girls don't plan on going out alone, do you?" Her eyes switched suspiciously back and forth between Cassie and Sheila.

Both girls shook their heads. Cassie felt guilty. She reminded herself that she had no reason to feel guilty —but they *did* want to see what Lyle was doing.

Sheila gave her a sign across the table that meant, "Let's go," but Cassie *had* to help with the dishes before she could enjoy herself.

At last they were alone, ambling toward the main campground. At the turnoff to Fossil Rocks, Sheila plopped down on the grass.

"Mom won't let us go canoeing, especially on the back lake," said Sheila. "We'll have to rent the canoe today, hide it, and sleep out again. Then she won't know in time to stop us."

Cassie traced ant trails on the ground with a stick. At last she responded, "I don't like deceiving your mom."

"You have a better idea?"

"Uh-uh-yeah! Let's just ask to go fishing."

Sheila jumped to her feet. "Right! The canoes come

with life vests. We'll make a big deal of it—rent fishing poles and buy bait and everything. Isn't this convincing? 'Mom, we've come to the lake for years, and never once did I get to go fishing.

" 'Please, Mom. While Cassie's here? We'll ask Mr. McLaughlin for the best life vests he has. What's the worst that could happen? If we fall in, we'd just paddle to shore and walk home.'

"That'll get her! It'll work! I know it will. Mom's great on experiencing things."

"Don't be too convincing," Cassie warned, in sudden panic. "We don't want your mom to go along."

"I can pull this one off!" boasted Sheila.

Sheila will be first again, Cassie thought. Oh, well, so what! Cassie had waited in the background all her life. One more time wouldn't hurt. Anyway, waiting was much easier. In fact, it was downright—no! It was . . .

A flush spread over her face as she thought the word. Reluctantly, she acknowledged it. Waiting was often downright . . . *lazy!*

18 Two Dangers

Forward, pull back, forward, pull back, forward, pull back.

Pulling on her paddle took all of Cassie's strength and concentration. Sheila had persuaded Mrs. Jordan to let them go fishing. Now they were paddling at dawn to the same place where Lyle had disappeared.

Morning mist curled off the water and disappeared into a low ceiling of fog. Cassie's hair, now auburn from the sun, curled in tight rings that sparkled with beads of moisture.

Reach forward, pull back. Reach forward, pull back.

Ahead of her, the back of Sheila's life vest glowed orange through the fog. *Lean forward, pull back.* Sheila's body moved to the same rhythm, with her paddle on the other side. She hadn't spoken to Cassie since they pushed off. Cassie was reluctant to break the silence.

A fishing pole lay in the bottom of the canoe. Cassie nudged it with her toe. She felt guilty and told herself they'd fish later.

An extra drag on her paddle aroused Cassie. Sheila

had stopped paddling.

"There are stumps up ahead," she reported. "We'll have to ease the boat between them. Don't paddle. I'll guide it through and tell you if I need help."

"Okay," Cassie agreed. Already, the narrow craft was gliding between the first stumps.

"Push away from that old snag," ordered Sheila.

Cassie shoved a paddle against the black wood sticking out of the water. The rear of the canoe swung slowly around. Through the fog, Cassie saw the overhanging bank with its soil washed from the tree roots. The scrubby pines leaned outward, making the edge of the water black and brooding.

"It's foggy, but I think it was about here that Lyle disappeared," Sheila commented.

"Let's lie down, then," suggested Cassie. "How long shall we stay down?"

"I don't know," responded Sheila. "This will be our signal. I'll put my thumb up, like this, if we're going to get up. Otherwise, we'll stay down. And we won't talk," she added.

Lying there in the bottom of the boat, Cassie mulled over all the threads that twisted through their lives: the dead geese, Joseph and his story of fit and unfit animals, beasts with rabies, Mr. Armstrong and the article he was writing and his strange behavior, Samba with her scratches, Ace walking to Fossil Rocks and finding the feathers and bones, Old Grouse and his house in the woods and his guns and panther stories, Lyle following them and coming here and hiding—surely he was hiding—like this, down in the boat.

The boat rocked gently. Fog drifted past. Cassie

shut her eyes and listened to the fuss of morning birds. She lay still so long she began to feel drowsy. Cassie roused herself and leaned up on one arm to see what Sheila was doing. Sheila lay still, her eyes closed. Cassie rolled back and settled down for a long wait.

Time dragged. She was daydreaming about school when a sound like water splashing caught her attention. Maybe Lyle had a rendezvous with someone. Was that the sound of someone paddling out to meet them?

Cassie peeked cautiously over the side of the canoe. She gasped. *A bear!* The animal lifted its massive front feet and stood on its haunches. Its gigantic head swung back and forth. A fish in its mouth flapped rapidly. It couldn't be a bear! But it was!

Frantically, Cassie grabbed her paddle and started pulling the canoe back toward the center of the lake. The light craft lurched and tipped crazily.

Woof! The bear dropped to the water with a startled sound. Its heavy legs showered water in the air.

A scream stuck in Cassie's throat. She was speechless with terror.

The bear spun around. Water dripped from its shaggy rump as it disappeared into the pines, leaving behind a faint foul odor.

Cassie sank back, her knees suddenly weak and trembly. The canoe rocked.

"What was that?" asked Sheila, sitting up.

Cassie stuttered, "A-a-a bear! I just saw a bear!"

"You didn't!"

"I did! It was in the water. Right there!" Cassie pointed to the place the bear had been. "You must have been dozing. We'd better get out of here." She resumed paddling out into the lake.

"Come on! Help paddle," she commanded, but Sheila wasn't listening.

"He could have been watching animals," she remarked.

"Who?"

"Lyle. Maybe Lyle lay down so the animals would come to the water as usual. Maybe he wanted to see a bear or a deer. Maybe he wanted to see a panther." Sheila's blue eyes were big in her face.

"Hey!" exclaimed Cassie, "If there really are panthers here, Lyle may be looking for them."

"Do you think there are panthers here?"

"I didn't believe Old Grouse, but now I'm not sure," Cassie mused. "I thought there were no bears, but I just saw one. Maybe there are panthers here, too. How big are panthers, anyway? The book said one hundred—oh, I don't remember! Two hundred pounds?"

"Beats me," replied Sheila. "We could ask Old Grouse. He'd know."

"Let's get this canoe back and go and ask him," agreed Cassie. She was paddling vigorously, and Sheila finally began doing the same.

The fog was lifting fast, and they paddled into sunlight. Ten minutes later, they tied up the canoe at the island.

Mrs. Jordan was eating lunch at the picnic table. She asked, "Well, did you catch any fish?"

Sheila launched into a story about how far out they went and how they didn't even have a nibble.

Cassie listened, knowing Sheila was distracting her mother so they wouldn't have to tell about the bear and be grounded. She didn't say anything, but she felt vaguely guilty.

After they had eaten, Cassie suggested, "Let's go to Old Grouse's and ask him more about panthers."

Sheila nodded in assent.

They paddled the canoe back across the lake, turned in the padlock key at the office, and set out for Old Grouse's. A few minutes of brisk walking brought them to his lane.

"Let's sneak up on Old Grouse since we're here anyway. Remember, Ace said he was acting strange. Let's go around the back of the house and see what he's doing before we let him see us," proposed Cassie.

They pushed their way into the tangled briars and shrubs beside the lane. Picking their way bit by bit through tangled underbrush, they circled around to the back of the house and hid in a thick patch of wild raspberries that seemed to have several paths through it.

Old Grouse! Cassie saw him come outside. She held up a hand and motioned Sheila to be quiet. Sheila moved closer. Cassie felt the warmth of her body and heard the soft whistle of her breath.

Lyle! Lyle came out the door behind Old Grouse. Old Grouse was pointing his gun—*right at them!*

Cassie grabbed Sheila and pulled her to the ground. A bullet whined through the branches above. A torn leaf fell on Sheila's head.

Crack! Crack! Dogs began barking. Thumping and banging seemed to come from an old outbuilding.

Cassie ducked her head between her knees, then lay down. The earth smelled musty.

"There's a paper target on that tree, and we're right in line," whispered Sheila.

"I know," returned Cassie. "Lie flat until he's done."

Cassie lay with her cheek against the ground. She wanted to pull out the briars that had snagged through her pants and into her skin, but she was afraid to move. Shots rained all around. Finally, the shooting stopped.

Cassie pulled herself to her knees and raised her head in time to see Old Grouse hand the gun to Lyle. Lyle aimed and shot.

Sheila's hands were over her ears. Cassie tucked her head down and tried to be deaf to the volley of shots. Her heart pounded. What if Lyle missed and shot into the raspberry bushes? She didn't dare move. Lyle might think she was a wild animal and shoot her.

At last, there was silence. She could tell that Lyle was talking, but she couldn't understand him. Then Old Grouse bellowed, "No, boy! Don't try to save 'em! What do we need 'em for anyway?"

Again, Lyle's voice was muffled. Then Old Grouse's voice floated to her ears again, "I'm a-tellin' you, boy, it ain't safe. All them people runnin' round over there at that campground and them all unawares of danger. And you want to save the animals!

"Leastways, you can shoot half decent, now. You can defend yourself. But them two girls, them thar friends of yours— Ain't safe, them walkin' all over the place. You can't protect them all the time."

Old Grouse's voice faded away. Cassie raised her

head. The two men got in Lyle's truck, which roared off.

She stood up. Sheila scrambled to her feet, her wide blue eyes meeting Cassie's.

"What were they talking about?" wondered Cassie.

"Rabid animals?" asked Sheila. "Yes, rabid animals, that's what they were talking about! That's why the dogs are penned up. Lyle's been following us to protect us. Maybe he was checking on us the night he was outside our trailer window."

Cassie surveyed the woods and shivered. "We must go home before we meet any rabid animals," she decided. "I didn't know rabies was spreading that much, but the way they talked, there must be an epidemic."

She picked her way out of the berry patch and headed down the driveway with Sheila at her heels.

19 The Search

A five-minute walk down the lane brought Cassie and Sheila to the highway. They set out for camp.

Cassie scuffed a shoe and nearly tripped twice. How tired she was! Getting up before dawn for two mornings, seeing a bear, and being shot at—it all had exhausted her. When the camp gates were in sight, she sighed with relief.

Beep, beep, beee-ep! Old Baby! Ace drove past them and pulled to the side of the road. Sheila broke into a jog and Cassie followed.

"Where have you girls been?" Ace called, "I've been to the trailer three times today."

A log truck roared by, blowing dust and grit in its wake.

"Get in," Ace commanded, "before you get run over."

As he drove under the stone entrance to the camp, he informed them, "I have to work all next week. This is my last day off before you go back to Washington. I thought I'd spend it with you, but Mrs. Jordan didn't even know where you were. So I drove around looking for you.

"Just got done checkin' at Old Grouse's. Thought you might have gone there. But no one was there, not even Old Grouse. Where ya been?"

"At Old Grouse's!" admitted Cassie. "You missed the shooting."

"What shooting?"

"We were in the woods, and Lyle and Old Grouse were shooting target right toward us, and—" Sheila stopped short.

"And what?" prodded Ace.

Cassie drew in a deep breath. "We heard them talking. About rabies, we think. About Lyle trying to protect us. Lyle said a raccoon attacked Samba. Did I tell you?"

Suddenly she had a mental picture of the bear on its haunches. "Sheila, maybe they meant bears," she added. "Ace, I saw a bear this morning, really I did! Do you believe me?"

"I do. People have seen them. Once in a while, there is a picture of one in the newspaper. Were they talking about bears?"

"I don't know. Bears or rabies? Either one would fit. Old Grouse said not to save them. And Lyle was arguing—he must have disagreed."

"If he meant rabid animals, why would Lyle argue to save them?" asked Ace. "They'd go mad and die anyway. Now, bears—I know a lot of people around here who want to get rid of them. They're afraid, mostly. Some of the old people would be glad to see them gone permanently. I've heard Old Grouse say that."

They crossed the bridge to the tiny island. Ace pulled up to the trailer. Mrs. Jordan hurried to meet them, her forehead drawn into a frown. "Is Midnight with you?" she asked.

"No, we tied her up," stated Cassie.

"Then she got away. I haven't seen her for hours. I thought she must be with you."

Cassie looked at Sheila, then Ace. Concern was in their eyes. Rabid animals, a bear! Midnight was too friendly to know danger.

Faced with Midnight's disappearance, Cassie suddenly wanted to be free of all the secrets she and Sheila had been keeping.

She hesitated, then blurted out, "I saw a bear this morning. Near the bank of the back lake, where the black pines grow. We have to find Midnight. She wouldn't be afraid of a bear."

Mrs. Jordan face paled. "Are you sure it was a bear, Cassie?"

Ace broke in, "There really are a few bears around here, Mrs. Jordan. People I know have seen one."

"Then don't go into that forest alone. Let me think what to do."

"Mr. McLaughlin would help us," suggested Cassie.

"Yes!" Mrs. Jordan agreed. "Get Mr. McLaughlin to help."

"Jump in my car, and we'll go get him," offered Ace.

They raced toward the car. Mrs. Jordan called after them, "Come back and tell me if you can't find him."

Ace drove around the lake, bouncing in the ruts instead of easing over them as he usually did. When they reached the office, Cassie ran inside. Between gasps, she asked for Mr. McLaughlin.

The tall, blonde girl at the counter was maddeningly slow. She tapped her red nails on the countertop. At last, her fingers stopped and she reported, "He went with a ranger from the park service up to Fossil Rocks. Why do you want to see him?"

"My dog disappeared."

"Well, maybe your dog followed them. Is your dog black all over?"

"Yes. Did you see her?"

"She was running around here about the time they left. You should keep her tied up."

"We left her tied up, but she got away. Thanks for the help." Cassie sped back to the car.

"Well," asked Ace, "will he go with us?"

Cassie settled back in the seat, took a deep breath, and told herself to stay calm before she answered. "The counter girl said Mr. McLaughlin went to Fossil Rocks with a ranger from the park service. Midnight was at the office. She may have followed them."

"Fossil Rocks!" groaned Ace. "That reminds me. Mr. Armstrong went to Fossil Rocks. This afternoon, I saw him acting strange. He was dipping a rag in a bucket and smearing it over his truck. Grease or oil, maybe. I circled back still lookin' for you and passed his truck coming my way. What an awful smell when he drove by, like something dead! I watched him in the mirror and saw him turn up the trail to Fossil Rocks."

"Midnight would follow him," Cassie assured them. "Was Samba along?"

"No, she was tied up. I drove around to look. Guess she's not quite healed up from that raccoon."

Cassie winced. Talk of Samba's scratches alerted her to the danger Midnight might be in.

"You said Mr. Armstrong is a photographer, didn't you?" asked Ace. "Does he take animal pictures?"

"Of course, he does. He writes about them, too!" cried Cassie. "That's it! THAT'S IT! The mud on his face and his smelly truck are a camouflage to cover his smell. What ani—the bear! The BEAR! We have to get Midnight. If she followed Mr. Armstrong, she may be in danger."

"More likely she put *him* in danger," Sheila commented sarcastically.

Cassie ignored the comment. "What do we do?" She looked at her friends and saw the same question in their eyes.

Ace jingled the keys in the ignition. His eyes were on the black pine forest beyond the back lake. He whistled softly. "I think we've got it! Mr. Armstrong has to disguise himself some way. Hey, I'm goin' up there. Want to go along?" He nodded toward the mountain.

"We can't go up there!" Cassie exclaimed.

"No one's been hurt by a bear around here for a hundred years. Be sensible. There are three of us," reasoned Ace. "Now tell me, would a bear attack three of us?"

"It doesn't seem likely," Cassie hesitantly agreed. "But we may spoil Mr. Armstrong's shot. Maybe he has everything set up for his picture, and we come around and scare the bear away. And Mrs. Jordan said to come back if we can't find Mr. McLaughlin."

"Well, we know where to find Mr. McLaughlin," observed Ace. "And you want to find Midnight, don't you?"

Cassie sucked in her breath and told herself, *I'm always being cautious; take a chance.* She replied slowly, "Ye-s. We have to find Midnight. . . . Let's go. Are you with us, Sheila?"

She saw Sheila's knuckles shining on clenched fists in her lap. *Sheila's more afraid than I,* she thought.

"Sure, I'll go," agreed Sheila, "but we can't tell Mom we're going alone. She'd worry too much."

Ace turned the key in the ignition. The motor started, and he reminded them, "We won't be on the mountain alone. After all, Mr. McLaughlin and a ranger and Mr. Armstrong are already up there. We can come back if it seems too dangerous."

"Okay," responded Cassie. She thought, *This is what people mean when they say the die is cast. I'm afraid, but I can't turn back now.*

Her heart was pounding as they drove back around the lake. Ace turned up the road to Fossil Rocks, carefully straddling rocks and bumps. Cassie wondered if she should tell him to stop and let her out, but the prospect of walking back seemed worse. The thought of meeting a bear alone was terrifying.

Besides, she couldn't turn back. Something inside her had made a commitment to—to what? She didn't have time to think about it now. To live dangerously? No, that would be silly. She'd think about it later. A phrase shot through her head, *Afraid of her own shadow.* Maybe she was determined not to let fear control her.

Afraid of her own shadow? Afraid of my *own shadow?*

Cassie scooted forward on the seat, her eyes on the road. Two tracks of squashed wildflowers and grass reminded her that they were not alone. Twigs scratched on the bottom of the car. Her fingers hurt from gripping the seat. The road got rougher and steeper. At last, Ace stopped the car and they got out.

"This is it!" he declared. "This is as far as Old Baby can take us. Now, let's see. Which way would Mr. Armstrong have gone?"

"Wait!" Cassie cried. "Up there is a worn spot in the road, like tires spun or something."

They got out to look. Cassie stooped to examine the tracks. "The tracks go forward. No, the tracks go to the side. Now wait a minute!"

Ace was thinking aloud, "There are two sets of tracks, Mr. Armstrong's and Mr. McLaughlin's, but which is which? No way to tell. Which way should we go?"

"Let's try calling Midnight first," proposed Cassie. "Maybe she'll come to us." Cassie cupped her hands around her mouth and called, "MIIIIII—I-D-NIGHT!" again and again.

The three friends leaned on the car and waited. Then Ace yelled for Midnight. The echo of his voice came back empty.

They were quiet, listening. A bumblebee droned in front of them. Cassie heard a soft clattering noise beside her. Sheila's teeth were chattering, and her braces were clicking together.

Cassie breathed a silent prayer: *Lord, give me courage, and keep us safe.*

20 Beware of Shadows!

Ace spoke softly in a calm voice. "We can't wait here forever. Mr. Armstrong's truck is probably parked at the rock ledge. Then he'll walk to the dark woods. I say we go that way." He pointed straight ahead.

Cassie took a deep breath, gathering courage to disagree. "But tracks go to the side, too. Right here is where we found the bones and feathers. Mr. McLaughlin and the ranger may have gone toward the great oak, the one Mr. McLaughlin said was the biggest oak of all—somewhere in the direction those tracks go. I say we look there first."

She pointed toward smashed ferns beside the road. Glancing toward the black, jagged pines ahead, she fervently hoped she wasn't wrong. The thought of entering the pine forest made her stomach knot.

Ace picked up a small stick from the ground and held both hands behind his back. "Pick a shoulder," he told Cassie. "Stick in my hand, we go up the rock ledge. No stick, we go sideways."

Cassie tapped Ace's left shoulder. He opened an empty hand.

"We go sideways," Cassie announced.

"I'm not going," moaned Sheila. "I have a headache. I'll wait in the car for you."

Again Cassie heard her teeth chattering. Sheila's face was ashen. Cassie was amazed. Sheila afraid? The car door slammed behind her.

Ace held out a thick, fallen branch to Cassie. "Here, take this, just in case."

"In case of what?"

He didn't answer. He fumbled about on the ground and came up with another stout stick, which he thumped on a rock, disturbing several bees in nearby flowers. They buzzed angrily.

The bumblebees buzz in the flowers, and it's an afternoon like any other afternoon, thought Cassie. She felt detached from reality, as though she were in a movie, acting out a script in which the heroine had just died, leaving her to play the leading role. It was a dreamlike movie in which close-up shots made bumblebees swell to fearful proportions. She, now the star, would face them alone.

She pulled herself back from such self-hypnotic thoughts. She was only Cassie, looking for her dog. *Midnight, come back!* her mind cried.

"If anything happens, don't panic," instructed Ace.

She nodded. Ace led the way into the woods. Her eyes searched every stump and shadow ahead. Ace moved forward, then stopped, looked about, and moved on again. They followed the tracks of squashed grass, stopping often and making every move cautiously. The toe of Cassie's shoe scattered a mound of delicate, silver-gray bones. Cassie shivered. She thought, *It's so quiet. Why don't the birds sing?*

A clump of elderberry bushes with seedy berries hanging in near-ripe clusters stood in an open spot. The tracks skirted it. *A bear could hide in there.* She saw Ace eye it warily. He led the way around, at a distance.

She saw Mr. Armstrong's truck first. It was on the far side of the bushes, nearly hidden by broken elderberry stems and tall grass. Cassie moved forward quickly and caught Ace's arm. When he turned, she pointed. He nodded, and she knew he saw it. They went on. Neither spoke, but relief slowed her pounding heart.

The tracks ended. From there, a single broken path through ferns pointed the way deeper into the forest. Cassie was encouraged to think of Mr. Armstrong ahead of them. She stepped forward, but Ace pulled her back and stepped in front. Cassie couldn't argue aloud, so she let him go ahead. A rotten smell made her gag. Could it be coming from the truck, as Ace had said?

The forest was ominously still—not even a bumblebee buzzed. Cassie knew she was afraid, more afraid than she'd ever been in her life. She assigned herself the task of keeping calm and counted her heartbeat by the pulse in her neck. Sweat dripped from her chin.

In spite of their careful walk, dried leaves and twigs rustled and cracked. The oaks seemed to be increasing in size as they probed deeper. Then Ace pointed to a tree. Cassie knew immediately that it had to be the great oak Mr. McLaughlin told them about. Its immense trunk was crowned with a low structure of wide-spread branches. There was an elderberry thicket under that oak tree.

Wait! A thicket wouldn't produce those clusters of berries in the deep shade of the tree. But how? . . . Maybe Mr. Armstrong made the thicket with branches from the place he'd parked his truck. Ace had stopped, and he, too, was studying the thicket.

A heat wave seemed to wash back from the tree, bringing the stench of a dead animal. Cassie held a hand over her nose, but there was no way to shut out the smell. She stared at the thicket, becoming more and more certain that it was made of cut branches— probably put up by Mr. Armstrong to hide him and his camera. In front of the thicket was part of a carcass, a bit of tan hide, and the bony ribcage of—a deer? She couldn't tell.

Fear clutched her. Perhaps they stood between a mountain lion and his prey. Was Mr. Armstrong in the thicket? She searched the forest on all sides and behind her, then turned again to the thicket. She tried to make out a camera lens between the leaves, but she could see nothing.

Her eyes traveled to the top of the tree where leaves seemed to move. Was Mr. Armstrong in the tree? A squirrel? Or was motion caused by the same breeze that brought the smell?

The tree trunk looked black through a break in the leaves. She heard no sound, but there was some movement farther down the tree. Ace stood beside her. Now the leaves were motionless. She strained her eyes to see. Something black—was it a bear cub? She looked behind them, uneasily, for an angry sow bear.

There! Leaves rustled over the man-made thicket. The black spot disappeared. The whole tree seemed to shiver and shake.

"Mr. Armstrong may be in the tree or—well—whatever's in the tree, it's big," whispered Ace. "Only something heavy would weigh a branch down that much."

The branches moved again, parting only for a second, then closing. Cassie gasped! In that second, she glimpsed a giant black cat. It had to be a cat—the long, curving tail, and the arching line of the back.

Ace whistled under his breath. "A panther!" he murmured. "If Mr. Armstrong is in that thicket, the cat's right over his head. Surely he sees it!"

"What should we do?" Cassie whispered. "If Mr. Armstrong knows it's there and we scare it away just when he's ready to take a picture, he'll be angry. But if he doesn't know, it could jump on him or attack him. Mr. McLaughlin's probably ahead on the road. Should we try to find him?"

"You go. I may be needed here," Ace muttered.

21 Shooting to Kill

Cassie *had* to find Mr. McLaughlin. She *had* to get help. Her goal to find Midnight passed through her mind again, but that faded in comparison to the danger to Mr. Armstrong.

She backed slowly away, keeping her eyes on the tree for another glimpse of the big cat. As her distance from the tree widened, she checked the forest in all directions.

Thump, thump, thump! Her heart and lungs seemed to have fallen into her stomach, making her nauseous. She had never felt her heart pounding like this before. The farther she got from Ace, the more dangerous the forest seemed. *Thump, thump, thump!* She forced herself to take a deep, slow breath. Cassie gripped the stick Ace had given her, took a watchful sideways step, and continued her retreat.

When she reached the truck in the elderberry patch, she decided it was safe to run. She flew down the trail. Cassie would get back to the car and ask Sheila to go with her to the rock ledge to find Mr.

McLaughlin. Two would be safer than one. Sheila would *have* to go.

She tripped on a root. Her knee scraped on a rock, and one hand was hot from sliding on the ground. No time for pain! She jumped to her feet and plummeted on through the ferns.

Rounding a scrubby pine tree, she saw Lyle in her path but couldn't stop. *THUD!* The top of her head hit Lyle's mouth. The impact threw her on her back on the ground. She lay senseless for a moment.

Then Lyle's face swam above her. She felt blood trickle from her forehead. A tongue licked it away, and an eager black face dripped saliva on her. Midnight! Relief flooded over her, but even Midnight could not stand in her way now.

Cassie jumped to her feet and cried, "Sorry! Lyle, there's a panther in the great oak." She wiped blood and saliva from her face, then wiped her hand on her clothes, talking all the while. "We think Mr. Armstrong's under the tree. Where's Mr. McLaughlin? Did he go up the rock ledge? Where, Lyle? Where is he?"

Lyle's mouth was bleeding, too. He seemed half-stunned, shook his head, and wiggled a tooth back and forth. Just then, Cassie saw Old Grouse coming through the ferns. He had a rifle in his arm, and his old body jerked along with unaccustomed vigor.

Old Grouse spoke a garbled sentence, and Cassie understood only "danged cat."

Lyle, recovering, raised his hand in a stop motion. "Say it again," he requested.

The old man pulled himself together to ask, "Where is he?"

Lyle pointed toward the lake.

Cassie blurted out, "No, he isn't. He's in the biggest oak tree." Too late, she realized Lyle was trying to distract the old man.

Old Grouse let out a howl of anger and launched into a fit of scolding. "Ya got to kill him! Ya can't scare the badness outa him. Now, y'all stay back until I git under the tree and git my rifle set on him. He'll stay treed a long time, but if you shoot before the aim is right, he'll leap out'n that tree right over our heads and be gone. No, sir, the aim's gotta be right the first time. Told you I shoulda brought my dogs. Let's go!"

The old man strode forward. Lyle grabbed his arm and pulled him back. "I said, we don't kill him. There are other ways."

Anger flashed in Old Grouse's eyes. "Let me go." He threw Lyle's hand off his arm.

Lyle grabbed the gun. Old Grouse yanked on the barrel to free it from Lyle's grip. As the rifle swung away from Lyle, Lyle's feet slipped down a slanted mossy rock. Cassie heard a cry of pain. The old man ran toward the big oak tree in leaps surprisingly spry for one not used to leaving his kitchen.

Cassie saw Lyle crawl to his knees. *He will be okay soon,* Cassie thought. She suddenly sympathized with the animal in the tree and was amazed at her feeling for the cat. After all, she was almost sure it had killed the geese.

She turned around and ran after Old Grouse. A string of related thoughts raced through her head at lightning speed as she ran: *Lyle is right. Animals eat each other. The cat eats to live. What difference does it make if it eats a doe or a goose? It hasn't harmed any people. Shoot the panther from prejudice and fear, and people become lower than animals. One shot from Old Grouse's gun might end a species forever.*

Cassie had to stop Old Grouse.

Hoping she'd scare the panther off, she screamed at Old Grouse, "Don't shoot him! Please, don't shoot!"

Recklessly she raced headlong after him. If she could just get in front of Old Grouse, she could stop him. He wouldn't dare shoot her. Midnight shot past her, straight as an arrow after the old man. Faster and faster Cassie forced her legs to take her. Her lungs ached. She leaped over fallen logs and raced on, speeding past the elderberry patch without thought of a bear.

The distance was shortening between her and Old Grouse, but not fast enough. Cassie heard Lyle running behind her. She yelled into the wind, hoping that someone would hear, "Stop him! Please! Stop him!"

Midnight was yapping wildly under the tree before Old Grouse got there. The old man charged right into the elderberry thicket under the mighty oak. The thicket seemed to disintegrate. Branches flew here and there, baring Mr. Armstrong, who tried to grasp a bucket but missed as he jumped aside. Red liquid flew from the bucket, carrying the unmistakable smell of rotten blood with it. Old Grouse, the only one left under the tree, sighted along a rifle barrel pointed straight up.

The old man was still aiming his gun upward when Cassie tackled his legs from behind. As she ran into him, she clutched his leather boots, shut her eyes, and held on. He fell forward. She heard shots as he hit the ground. They were followed by a strange pop that she'd never heard before, like a cork popping from a giant bottle. She flinched, squeezing her eyelids shut so tightly that her eyes hurt. The man's boots slipped from her hands.

The smells of gunpowder and leather boots, of rotten carcass, and a strong smell that was the musk of the cat rushed into her senses. The musk? She knew its maleness without being told. But her concern was for Old Grouse. She pushed herself to her knees, her eyes still shut, not wanting to see the old man's shattered body. Cassie hadn't meant to hurt him. Her mind screamed, *I've killed him. To save a panther, I've killed a man. Why? Why didn't I think about his gun going off?* Her terrified mind added, *I'll be in jail for murder!*

There was noise and confusion all about her: Mr. McLaughlin's voice, a strange voice, Lyle's voice, Mr. Armstrong's voice, Midnight's barking, then Old Grouse yelling, "Did I get him? Dang it! Kill that cat before he gets away."

Relief flooded over her. Old Grouse was alive.

Still on her knees, she opened her eyes and looked up into the tree—just in time to see an enormous black cat with glowing eyes half-leap, half-fall toward her! Terrified, she shut her eyes and screamed.

22 The Cat Comes Back

The weight of the cat hit her full force, knocking her to the ground. Screaming hysterically, Cassie covered her face to fend off its claws, then scrambled to her feet, still screaming. She was brought to her senses, not by attack, but by Lyle's arm around her shoulders and his steady voice saying her name, "Cassie. Cassie. It's over, Cassie. Stop crying. It's over."

Shaking uncontrollably, she turned toward him and clung for a moment, sobbing. Then she pulled herself together and stepped back.

The noise and confusion ceased. A man in uniform knelt on the ground, his back toward her. Standing, looking over the kneeling man, were Ace and Mr. Armstrong, and—Mr. McLaughlin? When had Mr. McLaughlin come? Where was the panther? Had she been unconscious? She was confused.

Cassie heard mumbling behind her. Old Grouse was nursing his shoulder. Seeing her attention, he grumbled loudly, "An' that skinny girl tackles like a football player. Shouldn't let girls in the woods. Never know what they'll do. Ain't safe."

She turned to Lyle. "What happened?"

"The ranger shot the cat with a tranquilizer dart. You threw the old man's aim off, and he shot into the air."

"But how—?"

"I don't know, either—yet. The cat's on the ground."

Cassie stepped forward and looked over the shoulders of the man in uniform. On the ground lay the panther, its coat gleaming as black as crow feathers. The uniformed man—a ranger—pulled a hypodermic needle from its body and stood up. Turning to Mr. McLaughlin, he announced, "Well, Bob, you did it. You proved the black panther exists, unless this one turns out to be someone's pet."

"He's no pet!" declared Mr. Armstrong. "I've got pictures to prove that. He came after me once, about the middle of the summer. Lucky I had Samba with me. She stopped him, but she still has scratches to show for it."

He looked at Cassie. "Sorry for yelling at you that day. I was really upset."

Cassie remembered—on the way back from the showers.

Mr. McLaughlin added, "And if Cassie's dog hadn't coaxed us down from the pine forest to this tree—hard to say what would have happened. That dog sure can run! Before we reached the tree, you wouldn't believe how many times she ran back and forth, between us and the tree."

The ranger nodded toward Mr. Armstrong. "You'd

be a mess—maybe dead—if these kids hadn't been looking for you. As it is, you just—" He searched for the right words. "You just stink!"

Everyone laughed. Cassie looked around. Mr. Armstrong was splattered with red from head to toe. Old Grouse was slightly spattered, too. Cassie examined herself. She, too, had a few spatters.

"What *is* that stuff in the bucket?" wondered Ace.

"Blood from the butcher shop," replied Mr. Armstrong. "I hunted cats for three years without success. I thought there had to be a way to bring them close. So this year, I made their hunting easy. I tried to think like a cat—which made my truck and me stink like a carcass."

"Did you know the panther was in the tree?" Ace asked.

"No. I thought he hadn't shown up today."

While they were talking, Old Grouse moved in closer. Now he warned, "Ef you don't take care of that critter now, he'll come awake and give a fight like you never seen. His tail's a-twitchin'."

The ranger whistled. "I already gave him a heavy dose, but he's a huge cat. I'll give him a booster, and then we'll get him out of here."

Still somewhat confused about what had happened, Cassie turned to Mr. McLaughlin. "Were you and the ranger looking for the panther, too?"

Mr. McLaughlin explained, "Lyle first saw the panther this spring. I reported it to the authorities, but no response. Meanwhile, Mr. Armstrong moved in, and the panther seemed to be getting bolder. I saw it take a goose one morning. I finally called my friend here."

He nodded toward the ranger. "I told him it was urgent. He came with the tranquilizer gun today."

The ranger gave the panther a booster shot to keep him down. Then he stood up, smiled at Cassie, and said, "We went to the rock ledge first. When we heard you calling your dog, we started down. We were almost here when you started yelling. This man's gun went off and missed. I shot the tranquilizer that brought the panther down."

The ranger shrugged off a backpack and opened it. He pulled out a tight roll of nylon netting, shook it out, and spread it on the ground. Cassie was amazed to see such a large net come from such a small pack.

"Okay, men! Help me get this fellow on the net," commanded the ranger. The men, all but Old Grouse, pulled and lifted the cat onto the net.

"Now, roll the sides of the net in like this," the ranger instructed. "We'll carry him out on this." He motioned to Lyle. "You and the photographer take that side." He turned to Ace and said, "You can help me on this side."

"My truck's close, over in the elderberry thicket. We can put him on the truck to take him out," offered Mr. Armstrong. He grunted as he bent over to pick up the animal.

As the men lifted the panther and started off, Cassie called, "Mr. Armstrong! Your cameras!"

"I'll be back for them," Mr. Armstrong assured her.

Cassie and Mr. McLaughlin followed the men. Old Grouse lagged behind. Cassie looked back and saw him slyly give Midnight crumbles of food from his pocket.

"What will the ranger do with the panther?" Cassie asked Mr. McLaughlin.

"He said he would relocate him far from the campground. This is the first panther the park service has ever captured. They've had lots of reports of sightings, but nothing to prove the animal even exists. Sure, they knew it was here in the 1800s, but the settlers were so angry about their dead cattle that they killed every panther they could. There must have been only a few of the big cats left in the wildest places, and it's taken them all these years to make a comeback."

"If he relocates the panther, will it return?" wondered Cassie.

"I called a private cougar research organization in Baltimore. They claimed cougars roam about from year to year but come back to the same spot every several years. So it probably will return, sooner or later," predicted Mr. McLaughlin.

The men had reached Mr. Armstrong's truck. Cassie watched them lift the animal onto the truck bed.

"Wow! This baby must weigh two hundred pounds!" exclaimed Ace.

"Must be close to that," agreed the ranger.

He turned and held out his hand to Mr. McLaughlin. "Well, Bob, you've finally done it—captured a real live panther. We'll photograph this animal. I know you have pictures of him, Mr. Armstrong, but we'll want our own photos to prove he exists. Then we'll weigh and measure him. Before releasing him, we'll likely give him a radio transmitter so we can track him. If he returns, you'll have to call me again. Don't try to fool around with him yourself.

"And you, Mr. Walker—" The ranger made a point of staring directly at Old Grouse. "I *will* have you arrested if you try shooting one of these animals again. They're protected by law. You can thank this girl here"—he motioned toward Cassie—"for tackling you and throwing your aim off, or I'd be taking you in *with* the panther."

"Don't know why a man can't protect himself against nasty critters like that cat," Old Grouse muttered. "Thinkin' the panther don't exist no more! Well, that do beat all! They've always been around. They're just mighty sneaky. Go off into the forest every oncet in a while and disappear for a year or two, but they'll be back. That big feller there on the truck will be back within two years, mark my words."

Old Grouse, disapproval stiffening his back, marched off down the trail. Mr. McLaughlin swung himself onto Mr. Armstrong's truck and rode out along with the ranger and the cat. Ace, Lyle, and Cassie walked toward Fossil Road, each lost in thought.

Cassie heard the roar of Mr. Armstrong's truck taking the ranger to the rock ledge where his vehicle was parked. When they heard the engine of the second vehicle, they knew the ranger had reached his truck. By now they were nearly out of the woods.

23 End of Summer

As Cassie, Ace, and Lyle came in sight of Old Baby, the car door flew open. Sheila rushed to meet them. "They took a panther up the road! Toward Fossil Rocks! On Mr. Armstrong's truck. Did you see it? Cassie, did you? Did you?"

"See it? She felt it! It jumped . . . no, it fell right on her." Ace began to tell Sheila everything that happened. He was almost finished when his voice was drowned out by noise from the trucks coming back from the rock ledge. The ranger came first with the caged panther in back, still lying down. Mr. Armstrong's truck followed.

As the trucks disappeared down the road, Lyle spoke softly, "Cassie, would you ride back with me?"

Cassie hesitated, surprised. After thinking of Lyle as possibly dangerous, she had to readjust her mental glasses. Her eyes met his. He looked shy and self-conscious, not aggressive and dangerous at all. Besides, he was still dabbing at a bleeding mouth.

"Okay," she responded with a laugh, "since we *ran*

into each other out here! . . . Sheila, Ace, I'm riding back with Lyle. We'll come straight down to the trailer, won't we, Lyle?"

"Sure."

Cassie hopped into his truck. Lyle started it and paused for Ace to go first. As they waited, Cassie apologized for knocking his tooth loose, then asked, "Why were you outside our trailer that night, the night we saw your head?"

"I wanted to make sure you and Sheila were safe, with Sheila's Mom and Dad gone and everything. That night I was scared, myself. Didn't you hear the panther scream? I tried to see if you were safely inside."

"That screaming was the panther?" Cassie was amazed. It had sounded like a person. "We weren't scared of the screaming, but we sure were scared of your head outside the window!"

Lyle chuckled, then explained, "You see, the morning you came here for the summer, Mr. McLaughlin sent me to your trailer to turn on the electric and water. The panther was there with the goose in its mouth. I don't know which of us ran faster! It dropped the goose and ran. I ran too! I went to find Mr. McLaughlin, but he was gone for the morning. I drove my truck back to the trailer. I couldn't see the goose or the panther, but I didn't get out to look. No way!"

"Midnight pulled the goose from under the trailer, in the back where the pilings are, so the panther must have come back and dragged it there," Cassie explained.

Lyle eased his truck through the ruts, following Old Baby. Through the open window, Cassie heard the rattle of the rusted truck body.

"Do you chew Wild-Nut gum?" asked Cassie, remembering the clue which had first made them suspicious of Lyle.

"Sure. Why?" asked Lyle. He pulled a pack of gum from his pocket. "Here, have some."

Cassie took a stick of gum and unwrapped it, then asked, "Were you outside our trailer really early the first morning we were here?"

"Yes, I was scouting to see if the panther had come back. I was there late—" He hastily interrupted himself. "I was there a lot, checking on you."

"You started to say you were there late. Finish it. I hate for people to make me curious and then not tell me something. What happened when you were there late?"

"I wasn't going to tell you this, but several times I parked my truck close by and just watched. Twice I saw the panther leap from that big oak onto the trailer roof and then down to the ground."

Cassie drew in a deep breath and let it out slowly, her eyes wide. "Whew! If we'd have known . . . so *that* was the thump on the roof I heard! Why didn't you tell us about the panther?"

"Believe me, I almost did several times, but Mr. McLaughlin said that maybe the cougar would just move on, and there was no point in scaring all the campers. There had never been a cougar attack on people in his lifetime. So he asked me not to discuss it and to help guard the campground. He reported it to the authorities, but no one came to help. Finally, he called his old friend, Ranger Evans, who's stationed fifty miles away. He came right away."

They were nearly to the trailer. Lyle pulled in and parked beside Old Baby. Cassie reached for the door, but Lyle wanted more time with Cassie. "Wait! . . . Don't get out yet. I want to tell you how much I admire you, Cassie. You saved that panther's life by tackling Mr. Walker—the man you call Old Grouse.

"You see, I went to his house because I heard he knew a lot about panthers and guns. He taught me to shoot. It seemed like a good idea at the time—strictly for defense on my part—but the old man was determined to go panther hunting. So then I had two problems—the old man and the panther."

"We knew, Sheila and I. We were in the woods and saw you shooting target. But why did you go out in the canoe that morning?" Cassie wondered.

"Thought I might see the panther come down to drink."

"That's what we guessed. A panther or a bear."

Silence hung between them. Cassie unlatched the truck door.

Again Lyle blurted out, "Wait!" His face was flushed. At last he continued, "I know you're going home next week. Would you write to me, then? I'd like you for a special friend. I like your courage."

"Courage!" exclaimed Cassie. "Me? The Shadow!"

"Shadow?"

Cassie was embarrassed. "Oh, that just came out. I think Sheila called me a shadow on the way up here. Then shadow things kept popping up in my head like 'she follows me around like a shadow,' and 'she's afraid of her own shadow.' Me? Courage? No, I just—

did what I had to do."

Suddenly, she remembered his question. "Of course, I'll write to you."

Lyle opened his door and got out. Cassie quickly leaped from her side of the truck. She added, "Maybe Sheila would like to write, too."

Lyle laughed, and Cassie wondered why.

"There you go again—looking out for Sheila. I don't want to write to Sheila. I want to write to *you!*" He looked in her eyes, and she gazed back at him. His eyes were the blackest eyes she'd ever seen. Then he suggested, "Could we walk down to the water before I go?"

"Sure."

Together they strolled to the water's edge. The geese were feeding there and came up to them cautiously, then surrounded them, pecking the grass around their feet. Cassie looked for Lila, the mate to the dead goose Midnight found.

She was no longer off to the side alone, but pecking with the others and exchanging pecks now and then.

Lyle sat down on a large rock by the water and patted a spot beside him. "Sit down."

Cassie sat down by his side. They were motionless. The open sky and the water filled Cassie with a deep peace.

At last Lyle broke the silence. "I want to talk to you about something. Something really hard for me to talk about."

He paused, and she looked at him. His jaw muscle moved with tension. *What is he about to say?* she wondered.

She waited. Finally it came out. "You know I'm part Indian?"

"Yes."

"Does that make any difference to you—about being my friend and all? I mean, some people think that whites should stay with whites and blacks with blacks and Indians with Indians. You know—they believe everyone should stay with their own kind."

Cassie hesitated. "Let me think about it a minute."

"As long as you like."

She thought, What would Sheila say? What would Mom say? What would Ace say? *What will I say? I don't know what any of them would say!*

Panic struck her as she realized that he was expecting an answer from her without consulting anyone. His question was forcing her to pull together all the threads woven through the summer and to braid them into something new called "Cassie's opinion." She wanted to run away and not answer, but she was—Cassandra—a whole person with an opinion. She searched herself for the answer that would come from deep inside.

Cassie remembered Joseph's story in which the animals were shown to Peter to teach him that no person is inferior to another. She reran in her mind the text on the bronze plaque at the entrance to the campground: "No man or animal drinks from a lake above another." Then she knew what to say.

"I, Cassandra Valin"—she paused for dramatic effect, smiled, and declared firmly, "will choose my friends as God made them, and I hope I have lots of variety in my life!"

Cassie saw pleasure wash over his face. They laughed together. She felt Lyle's fingers touch hers. Tentative at first, then gently his fingers wrapped around hers. She looked at his profile against the sky. Once she had thought him arrogant. Now the same cheekbones, nose, and lips looked—she couldn't think of the right word—stately?—noble?

His lips slowly curved in a smile. He looked at her and sounded out, "Mop-head!" There was playfulness in his voice.

Lyle untwined his fingers and rumpled her hair. "There!" he stated with satisfaction. "I've been wanting to do that since the day I first heard Sheila call you Mophead. Your hair is soft, just as I imagined. Mop-head!"

The way he said it, "Mophead" felt wonderful.

"I have lots of names," mused Cassie. "Mophead, The Shadow, Sheep."

"Sheep?"

"Yes, Sheila was Bo Peep and I was the sheep—following Bo Peep."

"I don't get that one!" he protested. "You're special, Cassie. You aren't a shadow. You're the real thing. And beautiful, too!"

Cassie wondered if she'd heard right. "Beautiful?"

"Yes, beautiful. That long mop of hair is the richest auburn I've ever seen. And you have nice skin—like books call porcelain! But you don't think so, do you?"

Cassie looked at him. "No, I . . ."

He held a finger to her lips. "Shhh. . . . Always enjoy a compliment."

As he walked her to the trailer, Cassie's heart was

singing. *Lyle likes me! And I am no longer Sheila's shadow, no longer afraid of my own shadow.*

"I have to get my mouth taken care of in the morning, but I'll stop to see you later," Lyle promised.

As he left, she waved good-bye. Then she stooped to pat Midnight, who had come to her side.

24 Going Home

The car was packed and waiting by the trailer. Sunday morning! Time to go home! The end of summer! Bill had already taken a load of things back to Washington.

Mrs. Jordan, Sheila, and Cassie had decided they would listen to one more of Joseph's stories before they left. They were nearly to the pavilion when Old Baby beeped behind them. Ace pulled the car onto the grassy parking space by the pavilion and hopped out. He fell in step beside Sheila.

Cassie looked at Sheila's happy face. She was glad for Sheila that Ace had come to see them off. Today she was also surprised to realize that she was no longer jealous of Sheila. Feeling peaceful inside was a wonderful feeling.

The music of the fiddles invited them inside. They found a picnic table and sat down. There was a sound at Cassie's side, and she glanced over to see Lyle seating himself beside her. She smiled a welcome, and he grinned.

"Came to see you off," he whispered.

How wonderful! she thought. When summer began, she wouldn't have imagined that anyone would want to see her off, especially not a boy!

Mrs. Jordan leaned across to welcome him, too.

Joseph, the storyteller, began a new story: "Long ago and far away, there was a potter who dug clay from the ground. He wet it and kneaded it and wet it until it was just right. Then he put the clay on a wheel.

"With his foot on a treadle, he spun the wheel around and around. While the clay ball on the wheel spun, he dipped his fingers in water and molded the spinning ball. To those who watched, his fingers seemed to do magic. The clay rose and fell, spread out and rolled in, until he made a container.

"Then he set it to dry in the sun. Soon, around him, hundreds of containers dried in the sun, each a little different from the others. When they were dry, the potter baked them in an oven.

"In this way, the potter supplied the needs of all the villagers. Some wanted to store oats and some fruits. Among the varied pots, each villager could find just the one he needed.

"All was peaceful until a villager decided that he had the ideal pot and began to brag to the others that his was best. Soon the pots themselves began complaining to the potter, 'Why didn't you make me like those pots?'

"And the potter said, 'I made you. Do I not have the right to make both a vase and a garbage pot from the same lump of clay? Are the pots not equally valuable although they serve different purposes? I am the one,

147

your maker, to whom you complain. It is my work you question.' "

Joseph stopped talking and silence fell. By now, Cassie was accustomed to his long pauses. At last he expounded, "God is the Potter. We are the clay. Shall we complain about the pots we are? No! Instead, let us rejoice in our uniqueness."

Cassie glanced over at Lyle, beside her. He was listening to Joseph. Looking at him reminded her of how he had called her "Mophead!" She reached up and touched her own hair. It was soft and springy. *My hair does feel nice!* she thought. *I'm a moptop pot! Wait till I tell Mom that tongue twister!*

Suddenly she could hardly wait to get home. She would grab Mom and hug her and say, "Hey! I made it! A whole summer without you! But I'm glad to be home."

Her eyes went to the water. She would miss the beautiful lake, the forests, and the sky. She would miss Lyle, too. But she would never forget this summer, the summer she ceased to be a shadow! And she would be back someday. Yes, she would be back!

The Author

Esther Bender is a teacher and writer who lives near Grantsville, Maryland. She has taught in public schools for twenty years and is presently a resource teacher. Since 1984, she has written more than a hundred published short stories, magazine and newspaper articles for children, and stories for children. She is a member of the Society of Children's Book Writers and Illustrators.

A 1974 graduate of Frostburg (Md.) State University, Bender received honors in early childhood education. In 1981 she earned a masters in elementary education with certification as a reading specialist. While at FSU, she studied reading under Dr. Judith Thelen, a past president of the International Reading Association and a speaker in demand at home and abroad. Since graduation, she has continued writing and taken courses in children's literature, fiction writing, and book writing for children.

Bender was born and raised close to Grantsville, near Springs, Pennsylvania, where she became a member of the Springs Mennonite Church. After high school, she married and moved to the Washington, D.C., area, where she attended Hyattsville Mennonite Church. Now she is a member of First Presbyterian Church of Cumberland.

In 1976, Bender discovered she had Parkinson's disease. Unable to function as a "normal" person, she was on her own personal ocean in the middle of a storm. At the time, she did not know that she would be blessed with new medications to control her disease and computer technology to open to her a whole new world of writing and publishing.

Today, Esther Bender and her husband, Jason, live quietly in a cedar house in the woods. They are both readers and computer "addicts." Esther writes on a Mac computer, and Jason on an IBM compatible. They share a laser printer. Esther says that computers make it possible for her to write when her hands are shaking. "I make lots of errors, but I fix them and go on."

Bender's short stories for children have been published in periodicals such as *Clubhouse, On the Line, Primary Treasure, Our Little Friend, Action, Happiness,* and *Story Friends.* Stories and articles for adults have appeared in local newspapers, *Christian Living, Purpose, United Parkinson Foundation Newsletter,* and other publications.

Esther Bender has written for and edited *The Casselman Chronicle,* a publication of the Casselman Valley Historical Society. She has done publicity for the National Pike Festival and contributed to the *National Pike Travel Magazine.*

With her computer and printer, Bender has self-published several family history booklets and earlier drafts of her fiction in private editions—at her own Lem'ntree Press. This is Bender's second book released for the open market. Her first book, *Katie and the Lemon Tree*, and her third, *April Bluebird*, are also published by Herald Press.

About *Shadow at Sun Lake*, Bender says, "When the dual-lane highway, now I-68, slashed through the mountains near my home, long-standing paths of wildlife were disturbed. Soon after the road opened, we were driving through a thick fog onto the entrance ramp when a black panther appeared right in front of the car. Its head rose above the hood, and its body stretched nearly the width of the car. We saw it only for a moment before the fog enveloped it."

Since that day, Esther has been collecting stories of local people who have seen panthers or cougars. She publishes them in articles or in booklets at her Lem'ntree Press.